记逝录

[美] 张明暐◎著　李　栋◎译

OBIT

VICTORIA CHANG

华东师范大学出版社

· 上海 ·

图书在版编目（CIP）数据

记逝录 /（美）张明瑄著；李栋译 . -- 上海：华
东师范大学出版社，2024 --ISBN 978-7-5760-5556-6

I. I712.25

中国国家版本馆 CIP 数据核字第 2025219LS0 号

上海市版权局著作权合同登记　图字：09-2023-1150 号

记逝录

著　　者	[美] 张明瑄	印 刷 者	上海中华商务联合印刷有限公司
译　　者	李　栋	开　　本	889 毫米 × 1194 毫米　1/32
策划编辑	许　静	印　　张	7.75
责任编辑	乔　健　梁慧敏	字　　数	108 千字
审读编辑	陈　斌	版　　次	2025 年 7 月第 1 版
责任校对	时东明	印　　次	2025 年 7 月第 1 次
装帧设计	卢晓红　郝　钰	书　　号	ISBN 978-7-5760-5556-6
		定　　价	78.00 元

出版发行　华东师范大学出版社
社　　址　上海市中山北路 3663 号
邮　　编　200062
网　　址　www.ecnupress.com.cn
电　　话　021-60821666
行政传真　021-62572105
客服电话　021-62865537
门市（邮购）电话　021-62869887
地　　址　上海市中山北路 3663 号
　　　　　华东师范大学校内先锋路口
网　　店　http://hdsdcbs.tmall.com/

出 版 人　王　焰

（如发现本版图书有印订质量问题，
请寄回本社客服中心调换或电话 021-62865537 联系）

摄影：Pat Cray

作者简介

张明睷　　1970 年出生于美国底特律，密歇根大学本科，哈佛大学硕士，斯坦福大学工商管理硕士，沃伦威尔逊学院创意写作硕士。出版获奖诗集 7 部、散文集 1 部、童书 2 册。现居洛杉矶。曾获洛杉矶时报诗歌奖、古根海姆学者奖等，入围美国国家书评人协会奖短名单和美国国家图书奖长名单等。

译者简介

李　栋　　多语作家、多语译者。首部英语诗集《橘树》获得芝加哥大学出版社新凤凰诗人系列首届新锐诗人图书奖，入围艾略特《四个四重奏》诗歌奖短名单。已成书出版的中文译作有《相伴》《新生》《魂与结》《安妮特》等。

给我的母亲和孩子们

目录

Contents

给悲伤以言语；无言的
悲痛

缝合失重的内心
并让它破碎。

———威廉·莎士比亚《麦克白》

我父亲的额叶——因中风于 2009 年
6 月 24 日不安详地死在了加州圣
地亚哥的斯克里普斯纪念医院里。
1940 年 1 月 20 日出生的额叶走过
了美好的一生。额叶喜欢当大哥，
它想再说说话，可有人给它套上了
袋子。额叶死的时候咬住了自己的
嘴唇，就像拉紧了一扇窗户。父亲
在他话语的葬礼上却不停地要说
话，他的爱穿过我的身体落在了并
不存在的地面上。我听到有人在跺
脚。身体和语言一样令人困惑：额
叶是在发脾气还是在跳舞呢？我拿
走了父亲的手机，他的话语在塑料
棺材里死去了。在他话语的葬礼上，
我们为我的流产争论不休。他说：
"这还不是一个真正的婴儿。"我无
话可说，跺着脚冲出门去摇醒那个
死婴。我想到了那个放下魔棒的急
救员，她在摸不到心跳的时候悄悄
地离开了房间。那时我终于明白了，
黑暗在无止境地坠落，黑暗并没有
吸入所有的色彩，而是吞下了所有
的语言。

我的母亲——因肺纤维化于 2015 年 8 月 3 日不安详地死在了加州阿纳海姆核桃村养老院她自己的房间里。她的房间是在 2012 年 7 月 3 日出生的。这个村也不是真正意义上的村子。也没有核桃树。只有切花。安宁疗护的护士默默地把听诊器放在母亲肺部的上方，等待它扩张。等待成了一种伤害。就像护士深吸一口气、闭上眼睛、呼出一口气说"对不起"的样子。血液是涌到了我的脸上还是指尖？护士说"对不起"之前或之后有没有再睁开眼睛？回忆是枪响之后的鸣响。我们试着回忆枪响却记不起来。就像是回忆在人死后站了起来，迈开了步子。

张明皑——于2009年6月24日在不知不觉中死在了I-405号高速公路上。她出生在汽车城,死在高速公路上也算死得其所。母亲来电告诉她父亲心脏病发作时,她的生活有了凹陷,她像不再汲水的燕子。这不是她第一次死亡。除了这次,她所有的死亡都带着褶皱。母亲的误判(其实是中风)并不重要,要紧的是张明皑得问要不要她开车去看额叶。母亲说"要"时,张明皑感觉自己并不想去。有人听到了这种感觉。因为父亲没有死,但失去了话语。在医院,她哭了,她再也听不懂父亲说的话了。之前,她并不理解父亲的病情有多残酷。这是她最后一次在这种疾病面前哭泣。她和自己的影子交换了位置,因为痛苦会改变形状,因为痛苦会偷偷发生。

张明皑——不情愿地死于 2017 年 4 月 21 日，在加州锡尔比奇一个凉爽的日子里。死的时候，她在从名为"日落"的护理院回来的路上，她常把护理院误称为"日出"。现在，父亲的麻烦成了她的，钉在了她的额叶上。她像个打字员般努力翻译他的麻烦，用小马车把词语一个接着一个运回来。马儿移动了，字母就会串成句子。马儿不想动了，小马车就会消失。字母拉上她跑进玉米地里。警察来了，用手电筒照亮玉米地并开始向字母射击，尽管字母已举起了双手。有时候，他们会向字母开两枪，以防万一。有时候，他们从背后开枪。我们打字母一次，那叫"打字"。打两次叫"刻字"。人死的时候，总会刻上字母。人死的时候，总会有种想和人说话的感觉，但装着所有话语的飞机正在划过天空。

语音邮件——死于2009年6月24日。父亲的语音邮件:"语音文字转录功能测试版(低自信),你好嗨哦我也许可以找到人来缩小汽车的尺寸OK我爱你。"语音文字转录功能测试版很自卑。它眯着眼睛徘徊着走进河里,回来的时候就失明了。语音文字转录功能测试版无法转录痴呆症。其实,父亲说的是"我会叠果汁",而不是"我爱你"。语言是扫帚还是被扫的事物?一看到"我爱你",我就感到有一只手在我的肺上绕了一圈细线再拉紧。因为父亲从未对我说过这样的话。在意识到错误的前几秒,我感受到的不是爱而是恐慌。我们阅读是为了承载文字,但我们和文字之间却隔着什么。直到死亡来临,理解和消逝将同时发生。

语言——死于 2009 年 8 月 1 日下午 2 点 46 分，死得灿烂而美丽。语言喜欢举手，一生都在提出问题。语言最喜欢扭曲别人说的话。语言最喜欢把世界变成白纸黑字，然后看人们试着把文字读出色彩。字母放手前在父亲的脑海中一掠而过。现在他的话语失明了，打上了褶皱，成了调度员、派送员和接收员。母亲弥留之际，我让大家伙儿都站在她的床边拍最后一张合影。我们中的有些人甚至还露出了笑容。因为死亡在停滞前不得安宁。有人说"多拍几张"。有人说"说茄子"。有人说"谢谢"。语言让我们失望。就像"摔断手臂"意味着手臂的骨头可能断了，但手臂本身并没有断掉，除非是截了肢。母亲说不出话来，但只有她的眼睛才是完全睁开的。

短歌

孩子们啊，我的孩子们，
到处都是苹果酱，
但不是给你们的。
帮人长大
又帮人死去，很奇怪。

*

我每次写下希望，
字母都会磨损散落。
满怀希望的诗人
好像从来没有做过我的梦，
好像从来没有过孩子。

语言——又死于 2015 年 8 月 3 日上午 7 点 09 分。我听闻母亲夜里难熬，于是雇了一个陪夜的护工。等我赶到时，那人已经不在了。这个护工有名有姓，却像个幽灵，把字母留在岸上，等我把字母拿回家时，它们已经变成了贝壳。"凌晨 2 点 33 分，无法呼吸；3 点 30 分，尖叫；4 点 24 分，平静下来。"我跪倒在地上，试着拾起字母，就像一个没有篮子的孩子去捡拾彩蛋。但每捡起一个字母，另一个又掉落，就好像在抗议对母亲之死过于简单的处理。我想让护工用我能理解的语言留下消息。"2:33，呼吸展开；3:30，呼吸急促如刀片；4:24，呼吸像一件晚礼服。"但也许是我错了，死亡就是死亡，每一场死亡都略有不同，但最后的一击都没有差别。就像皮肤对婚纱和雨水会做出相同的回应。

张明皑——死于 2011 年 6 月 24 日，享年 41 岁。但她的想象力却活过了那一天。她的想象力重达两磅，还能像哑铃一样被举起。她有次带父亲去了一条拱廊商业街。父亲找了个篮球机，就一个接一个地投篮。他用手抚摸着透明玻璃上自己的模样，就好像在监狱里探视过去的自己。在玻璃的另一边，像"堤岸""丑陋""异质"这样的词还没有消失。他想向过去的自己寻求帮助，但狱警不允许他传递纸条。篮球机嗡嗡作响的时候，他停了下来，眼神畸形而狂野。他向我招手，喊我死去的母亲去看他的得分。当影子附着在了错误的物体之上又拒绝放手会怎样？我走了过去，因为想要相信他。

未来 —— 死于 2009 年 6 月 24 日。作为过去的先驱人物，未来是当下的总统。你坐着。但未来要你的椅子。未来要求很高，感兴趣的不是脊柱而是脊柱能撑起的事物。未来对颁奖典礼感兴趣。未来对像奖牌一样掉落的花瓣感兴趣。未来对所有带"轨""迹""径""路"的词感兴趣，比如"终身制轨道""鹿的足迹""田径运动服"，却不想让你"脱轨"或"原路返回"。未来可能会被有特权的人抛弃。但有时候未来也会突然死亡。就像一位母亲去世时，第二人称也跟着死了，重生为第三人称的"我的母亲"。悲痛其实就是未来的缺席。就像一位母亲过世时，未来不再办公。留下的是地上跟暴力一样大的洞。

礼貌 —— 死于 2009 年 6 月 24 日，享年 68 岁。被中风谋杀，中风的画作最近在美术馆展出，两幅方形画布涂成白色，中间各有一把剪刀开着口指向对方。父亲中风后，母亲就不再把句子说完整了。鳕鱼的片段、野蛮人的语言，每一个音节都机械般地从她的嘴里飞到我父亲的洞里。也许这就是语言失灵的样子，向内的最后一口气，向外却没有了呼吸。一种永远屏住呼吸、不死的状态。肺开始衰竭的时候，她还能说出"你"，但说不出"谢谢"。我让她别对父亲大喊大叫的时候，她说："你不知道这是种什么感觉。"她说得没错。当语言离场，留给你的就只有口吻，留给你的就只有烟雾信号。我不知道她是在用自己的身体作木头。

我母亲的肺——在过去的某个时候开始衰竭。医生们绕开墓碑这个话题。谈到墓碑旁的灌木<u>丛</u>、墓碑<u>上</u>的字体。写讣告的人说，讣告是一个人成为历史的时刻。要是母亲从未讲起战争和她小时候的故事呢？这是否意味着一切都没有发生过？没有人坐在母亲矩形的小墓碑旁边，墓碑和大地平行。墓碑上的字要从上往下读。要是我在太空读不到呢？那是不是意味着她没有死？她是在太平洋标准时间早上 7 点 07 分过世的。比夏威夷时间早了三个小时。那是不是意味着在夏威夷她还没有死？但飞夏威夷要五个小时。这个时间差无法逾越。这种差距就叫悲痛。

隐私 —— 死于 2015 年 12 月 4 日。我的孩子带着一个写着"早日康复"的气球来到墓地。这次，彼得·曼宁躺在了母亲身旁。一个离她这么近的陌生人。在这块新墓碑出现之前，母亲的墓碑仍然是我的母亲，因为周围什么都没有。新墓碑的出现和墓碑的相似性意味着我的母亲也是一块墓碑而已，我的母亲也被埋在了墓碑下面。下葬那天，我请了位华人牧师。牧师说的很多话我都没听懂，因为说的都和食物无关。挖完土的男子们拿着铲子等在一旁。我看着他们的眼睛，寻找着溺水的迹象。我注意到一名男子的身后没有影子。他走开的时候，草还是直的，没有被踏平。他的铲子干干净净。我突然意识到这名男子代表着爱。

我母亲的牙齿——死了两次，一次是在 1965 年，因牙龈问题全被拔除。另一次是在 2015 年 8 月 3 日。她的假牙放在了车库的一个盒子里。她死的时候，我摸过、闻过她的假牙，觉得还听到了呜咽声。我把假牙塞进自己嘴里。但两副牙齿只让我感到更加饥饿。母亲死的时候，我看了看镜子里的自己，她的话语在我嘴边形成了一个圆圈，像甜甜圈上洒的糖粉。她的遗言是用英语说的。她要了听雪碧。我心想她最后思考用的是不是中文。我心想她最后的思绪是什么。我曾以为人死了，说过的话也跟着死了。现在我知道这些话会像香气一样散开，寻找可以附着的意义。母亲曾用浅口的小碗收集橘子花。每年春天，我都会从那棵树旁经过。我一直都认为悲痛是可以闻到的。但我不知道悲痛其实不是名词而是动词。它会移动。

我告诉我的孩子们，
希望就像一条蓝色的裙子，
它会转啊转，
男子们希望打开它，
把它拆开，让它受伤害。

*

我告诉我的孩子们，
有时我也可以怀有希望，
有时一切都会停止，
除了我对某人的爱，
还有逝去星星的光。

友情 —— 死于 2009 年 6 月 24 日，曾经爱过的，但不是挚爱。镜子赢了这场争斗。我现在被囚禁在镜子里。我所有的自我像一副扑克牌散落一地。的确，哀悼的人说着另一种语言。我和朋友们被纱布隔开。我会开车把自己送到家里去参加聚会。我会和自己闲聊，把酒洒在自己身上。聚会结束，我会开车把自己送回家。我和其他家长关于孩子的谈话在上楼时与我擦肩而过，在下楼时又重复一遍。母亲去世前，我会随便找个地方坐下。现在，我会找空桌子形象旁边空椅子的形象。形象就是一种距离。我的形象坐了下来。抑郁是套在心上的手套。抑郁是套在心的形象上的手套的形象。

步态——父亲的步态死于 2011 年 3 月 14 日。挺拔、轻盈、平足。玉树临风。现在却像砂纸一样拖着脚步。父亲为了省钱曾支起篮球网，把它装在从木材厂买来的木杆上。每投一次篮，木杆都会动一下，肉眼不能马上察觉到，直到我得移到车道边去投篮。现在，我避免使用分号。我寻找那些眼神不会跟随我移动的雕像，那种站在原地不动、身上能挂灯泡的人。问题是，父亲的大脑走得停不下来，而死去的母亲却无处不在。

逻辑——父亲的逻辑在大白天死于
2009 年 6 月 24 日。在那天下午被
谋杀。我挂起自己的寻人启事，倾
听树倒下的声音。风吹过树木的声
音叫做"微风动叶"。没有一个词能
指代风的译者。如果风是词，那树
就是感叹号。月光的长矛就是问号。
父亲没有意识到他说话总以介词结
尾。"矛盾是我跟（月亮的），矛盾
在于（月亮和我）之间，矛盾出在
（月亮上）。"要是他再也找不到介词
的宾语呢？就像雪会一直往下落，
如果没有送雪上西天的嘴唇。

乐观——死于 2015 年 8 月 3 日，是人行道上的慢性死亡。雨滴在什么时候接受了自己的坠落？是云在它身下收紧的一刻？还是地面刺穿它、打破它形状的一刻？在十二月，母亲让护工帮忙准备了一顿中式火锅宴。母亲说，这也许是她最后一个圣诞节了。我取笑她。她整晚对着父亲大喊大叫。我把一颗鱼丸塞到嘴里。我的乐观包住了整颗鱼丸，就好像鱼从未死过，从未被开膛破肚、揉成屈辱的形状。承认死亡就是要承认我们必须变成另一种形状。

野心——死于 2015 年 8 月 3 日，死得很突然。我把野心埋在了森林里，放在苦恼身旁。它们曾一起散步，直到野心把苦恼推下了堤坝。现在，父亲的脚踝上套上了一个环。他离房间门口太近，警报就会响起。他的野心促使他经常走到门口。警报响了，他就感到很苦恼。他记得想去找我家。他觉得可以找到我家。他的指纹早已从我家消失了。但有些罪犯会把手指放到电炉的丝盘上抹去指纹。这样就更容易找到他们。上个月，他们在马路中央找到了父亲，他安静得像一盏没有灯泡的灯，身体功能被遗忘，迷茫得像月亮。在动物园，一只巨大的秃鹰因失去了一支翅膀被关在了一个小笼子里。它仅剩的另一支翅膀就是悲痛。秃鹰头顶的一只飞鸟就是秃鹰的回忆和它的猎物，也就是未来。

椅子——母亲的一把绿色的椅子死于 2015 年 8 月 3 日。我们将椅子朝一个方向排成一排代表尊敬。围成一圈代表分享。叠起来代表圆满。悬挂在天花板上代表艺术。放在书桌前代表工作。母亲去世前，我把她所有的邮件都转到了我家。她订阅的商品目录仍然每天都会寄来。我想象她坐在椅子上翻看，挑选更多看起来款式一样的衬衫。我现在明白了，只有活着的人才会换衣服。上周，我带父亲去买裤子。我听到他和裤子吵架。他从试衣间出来时，裤子穿反了。两个口袋朝前，就像母亲的一双眼睛在嘲笑我，就好像在说："我早跟你说过。"父亲怒气冲冲，指着不合身的裤子破口大骂。我走进男士试衣间，捡起地上所有的裤子，因为有一条就是我失去的父亲。

你闻到了我的哭声吗？
哭声从另一个地方来。
是你在哭。
现在是你带来了一切。
既空虚又充实。

*

我告诉我的孩子们，
她们可以唤醒一切，
还没有到她们
死去的时候。但我又怎么知道？
我知道一位母亲死了。

眼泪——死于 2016 年 8 月 3 日。有次在去墓地的路上，我们在一家冯氏超市购买了鲜花和风车。已经过去一年了，死亡也不再那么鲜亮。我十岁的女儿把花完好地插在了墓碑前的一个窄口小洞里。不知怎的，她知道那个洞是用来做什么的，她知道我的母亲其实并不在另一头。突然，我们泣不成声。我曾多少次仰望天空，希望得到某种讯息，得到的却只有内容没有形式。我女儿跑回了车上。就像哀悼有很多种形式，就如同眼泪或风车。就像"干草堆"这个词永远不会让人联想起第二个画面。就像我们以为所有眼泪的味道都是一样的。就像我们的悲伤是复数，但哀悼则是单数。

回忆——死于 2015 年 8 月 3 日。死亡来得并不突然，而是慢慢地走过了十二年。我在想，人死的时候，会不会听到钟声，或是尝到甜味，或是感到有把刀像切薄片蛋糕一样把身体切成两半？见证母亲死亡的护工辞职了。她保存着记忆和影像，但现在一切都没了。在她有生之年，记忆都只属于她。她说，我母亲不能呼吸，二十秒过后就咽下了最后一口气。就像我曾想象与许多从未吻过的男子接的一个吻。我对母亲之死的回忆不可能是一种回忆，而是一种想象力，每次风吹过，叶子都会以略微不同的方式展开。

语言——死于 2017 年 3 月 4 日。它想以自己的形式尽可能长久地活下去，就像屋檐上的一根冰柱。我掀开父亲头上的屋顶，找到阳台站了上去。我大声地、慢慢地说着古根海姆这几个字。我们对面桌上的两位女士各自端着一盘随意吃到饱的雪蟹腿，已经是第四盘了。我一遍遍地重复着。两位女士不停地起身去拿食物，她们吮吸的声音就像是在吃一只熟透了的桃子。父亲终于开口了，他想看看"那本小册子"。今年，有艘太空飞船被派去在土星和土星环之间执行自杀任务。如果我可以站在父亲和他的大脑之间，我是不是也会自杀呢？如果有人指挥着飞船，那不就是谋杀吗？发回的照片是无声的。一张照片代表了逝去的一瞬。那么，每一张照片都是犯罪现场。当我们在某一刻记起死去的人，我们想起的是照片，而不是那个瞬间。

托马斯·特朗斯特罗姆 —— 死于 2015 年 3 月 26 日，享年 83 岁。他曾写道："我在自己的影子里 / 像一把小提琴 / 躺在黑色的琴盒里。// 我唯一想说的话在遥不可及的地方闪着光 / 就像当铺里的 / 银子。"父亲在中风前后都不可能写下这样的文字。我在想诗人的女儿们是否像我不喜欢去看望我父亲一样不喜欢去看望他。就像父亲握紧的拳头，就像他远在天边的思绪。就像他的话放弃了他的嘴，我每天把话捡起来，放回去，再把盖子拧得更紧些。有时，他抱怨却没人能知道他在说什么，我就想起小时候所有躲过的地方。还有每次我用自己的嘴捂住别人的嘴，让他们不能说话。

认可——死于 2015 年 8 月 3 日，享年 44 岁，是早上 7 点 07 分死的。"你能赚到多少钱"是我母亲对一切的回应。她常在自助餐厅用餐巾纸把玛芬蛋糕包起来放入她包里。我没有再见过那些玛芬蛋糕。我多么希望再看到那些玛芬蛋糕，看到蛋糕被她掰开时露出的松软的细丝。在一张照片上，母亲牵着我的手。那一年我九岁。我之后就再也没有碰过她的手。直到她去世的前一天。我喜欢很多我从未触摸过的事物：月亮、颤栗、母亲的心。她的手指粗糙得像包着塑料的树枝。她靠着吗啡睡下的时候，我给她一个一个地剪脚趾甲。她的脚趾甲不是小月亮，也不是通往某处的金色大门，而是我要剪掉的最后十个字。

有时候，我拥有的
就只有文字，写下了
就意味着文字不再是
祈祷，而是成了野兽。
别人可以猎杀它们。

*

你在我这里
什么都不需要，你已经
拥有了所需要的一切：
月亮、湖面的伤口、
我们不被追随的脚印。

秘密——死于 2015 年 8 月 7 日，如
释重负。葬礼上没有人知道母亲的
病情。没有人知道我父母的争吵有
多激烈。一张又一张华人面孔。我
把事情讲了。又讲了一遍。他们的
嘴巴像时间一样张开。红带子上的
汉字我看不懂。花茎和花朵说着话。
花突然低头看到腿不见了。后来，
我找到了一张照片，是前年母亲微
笑着和朋友们在家中的合影。没有
氧气瓶，鼻子里也没有插管。在她
生命的起点和终点之间，她一定是
把插管取了下来放在了柜子里。我
想象她内心惊慌失措，等着朋友们
离去。思维和言语像大雁般排成一
队又拆开。现在科学家说，人死后
大脑仍在工作，大脑的能量会突然
爆发出来。也许她听到了头顶大雁
最后一次拆开队伍的声音。或许我
吻她脸颊的感觉像闪电。

音乐——死于 2015 年 8 月 7 日。我用老照片配音乐为葬礼制作了一段视频。我选了无伴奏合唱《哈利路亚》。因为那不再是合唱，而是真正的哭泣。孩子们走进房间的时候，我假装在写作。其实我在翻看母亲的旧照片。她所有衬衫上的布料图案。她双手在胸前合十的样子。每张照片上都有的棕色小包现在放在了我的书桌底下。葬礼上，我姐夫老是把音量调低。他不注意的时候，我又把音量调高。因为我想让来参加葬礼的人都能明白我的感受。我不注意的时候，他又把音量调低。最后，有人把屏幕和扬声器都拿走了。但音乐还在回荡。这是我第一次体会到悲痛。

食欲——最终在家人的陪伴下，平静安详地死于 2015 年 6 月 21 日的父亲节。我们为母亲穿好衣服，将她推上轮椅。氧气机像野兽一样呼吸着。他们是养老院里仅有的华人。中间的桌子旁又喧闹起来，又是仅限被邀请者。像往常一样，我给母亲的盘子上装满了食物。她最喜欢的彩色布丁装在塑料杯中。我们起身离开的时候，她的食物还在餐盘上，像虫子一样闪着光。没有人去多想。有些瞬间就像一笔一画，只有在沧海桑田之后，才成为悬崖峭壁。死亡是我们共同的祖先。它不在乎我们与谁共餐。

食欲 —— 死于 2015 年 3 月 16 日。读研究生时，有一次在餐厅只有我一个人点了杯酒。我男朋友不喜欢这样，就停车把我扔在了市中心，让我自己走回家。看着橱窗里的童装，有条纹小帽子、粉色连衣裙，我想到了美好的事物。我转了一圈，想躲开黑暗，但让我转圈的却是黑暗。我躲进了一家塔可钟快餐厅。男收银员的嘴巴像个窄洞，脸颊上还有棕色的硬块。美丽得让我认定他就是死神。二十年后，母亲想在中午吃塔可钟。我跑出去给她买了一大包塔可卷。排队的人都不能理解我急切的心情。我把信用卡递给了一名脸上有棕色硬块的男子。他把袋子递给我的时候点了点头，好像他知道一切似的。母亲把嘴唇贴到塔可卷上，就像是最后一次狂吻某个人。

形式——死于 2015 年 8 月 3 日。我的孩子们搂着我母亲的相框入睡。是棱角分明的深灰色金属相框。我十岁的女儿把相框放进装骨灰盒的红色天鹅绒袋子里，还带着去度假。母亲的照片就放在曾装过她骨灰的袋子里。我们死的时候会以不同的形式被表象的表象所代表。回忆也是死者的表象。我穿过长廊寻找原型，却找不到她。在棕榈泉，沙漠让我失望。灰尘、沙子、砾石，到处是死去事物的碎屑，别人死去的母亲的碎片吹到我眼睛里，我又开始哭泣。天气变得过于乐观。泛光的游泳池就像一场审判。我自己的呼吸在溅起的水花和孩子们的笑声之间已不再是奇迹，而是简单的数学。

乐观——因单调乏味死于 2015 年 8 月 3 日。我姐姐飞回家之前都会和母亲一起哭一场。母亲只对我哭过一次,我说:"医生错了,你不知道还有多久——可能是一年,也可能更久。"她没有停止哭泣。我起身离开了房间。屋外,在三层楼下的大楼后面,有家人在院子里庆祝着什么。有皮纳塔、音乐,还有孩子们,他们在空气屋里暂时悬浮于地球上空。那年夏天,我们不在地球之上,而是在上面的一栋楼里来回踱步。城市里的人可能一辈子都不会真正接触到泥土。我真害怕他们的快乐会像蒸气一样从窗口飘走。我能听到打在皮纳塔上的棍子砰砰作响的声音,之前对幸福的期待现在被必然掉落的糖果所改变。现在,我闭上双眼,努力回忆砰砰作响中的乐观,还有一切事物的起源。

我不可能有底气地说
我会冲向公交车
把你从死亡中拯救出来。
一个女孩的好坏
取决于她的母亲，那又怎样？

*

去爱一个人
意味着承认灭绝。
我这样对自己说，
所以我不会坠入爱河，
所以火光只会照亮我一个人。

手——死于 2015 年 1 月 13 日。母亲的字迹已变得歪歪扭扭。身体跳下床。脚一纵从桥上跃起。手从不跳跃。手示意让人留步。手势加强了语言的效果。手是拥抱的最后一部分，而身体则承担了大部分动作。手擦去眼睛里流出的泪水。手在纸上写下大脑发出的信息。母亲去世后，我看到一张她已从急诊室搬到养老院的照片。她的鼻子里插着氧气管，我两个年幼的孩子分别站在两侧。她的双手把两个孩子的手紧紧抓在胸前，指关节的合唱还在回响，白色的石头将要被释放，很快就会像马儿一样溅起水花。

氧气 —— 死于 2012 年 3 月 12 日。起初是沉沉的绿罐子。然后是一台滚动大机器，不分昼夜地送出气体。母亲换衣服的时候得先把插管从鼻子里拔出来。她停下来喘气，就好像呼吸一直在运动，就好像呼吸可以被追赶。我不知道什么时候开始注意到母亲没有插氧气管时的恐慌，就像我们没有马上注意到一片叶子变红了或是一个帝国的崩塌。有一天，就这样出现了，就好像一开始就是那样的。就像安宁疗护中心的工作人员，拿着一沓文件、一包包药，还戴着沉默的花环。就像悲痛，就像悬挂在万物下方的耳环。就像悲痛需要氧气。就像它时不时地会起烟。就像我的悲痛会和我一起死去。就像开裂生长的鹿角。

理智——死于 2009 年 6 月 24 日，就像仿真的树刚被拆下来收好。父亲的话语从他的大脑中被取出仍在楼下。遥远，但又近在咫尺，就像你孩子身上的伤口，或是另一个房间里吹动的窗帘。这周，他又迷上了定时散步。这周，他不想等待其他更年迈但思维更敏捷的老人。理智的记忆还在，还知道怎么掌控。理智死了，决心还在。就像我父亲决心上午十点以一定的步速走路。就像无论大脑受不受控制他的身体都决心向前迈步，而他的大脑就是一双钉在地上的空拖鞋。

家——死于 2013 年 1 月 12 日。搬家五次里的第一次意味着箱子仍然乐观地认为会被打开，仍然笔挺，为自己的新形状而感到高人一等，扁平只是回忆。在新家，父亲在一次雷打不动的散步路上碰到了一位华人老者，是一位瘦骨嶙峋、满嘴树枝牙的老太，这样的人我母亲通常会因为她的出身而避而远之。那一年，她每天都来看望母亲，还会带些橘子、蔬菜和一名殡仪馆的销售人员。父亲出去转悠，让她们用中文聊天，也免得他不锻炼死得快。那老太用中文骂我父亲是"蠢货、笨蛋"。在葬礼上，她说："是上帝派我来帮助你母亲的。"我突然意识到父亲的话语是一把打不开的伞。母亲握着伞，不让风吹走。而这位老太就是风。

记忆 —— 死于 2015 年 7 月 11 日。我出差回来，母亲坐在床边，花白的头发下都是黑色的染发剂，就像记忆。床单被扔在角落，像碾碎的小鸟。护工已经一周没来了。父亲来回踱着步子，试着用手势说话。手承受了太大的压力。除了手，没有谁知道那一周发生了什么。母亲把大便拉在身上了。她平时用粉红色卷发机一根根卷起的头发上面到处都是。她矢口否认。还用中文骂我。我和我的孩子给她洗澡，她赤身裸体地坐在洗澡椅上，耷拉着脑袋，像是受挫的野兽。死亡仍然很抽象，可以从下水道流走。悲伤仍然不可分割。二十三天后，悲伤引爆，像五彩纸屑撒在我们头上。水抚平了母亲的头发，并开始淹没她的舌头。

二

让星星
垂直坠入它们黑暗的归宿，

让瘸腿的
汞原子滴入
骇人的深井，

你就是那一份
空间倚靠的坚实，让人羡慕。
你就是谷仓中的婴孩。

——西尔维娅·普拉斯《尼克与烛台》

我是矿工。灯光变蓝。

一群　肋骨　　　　　　把　我们的

卵子扯了下来　　　　剩下的　　是数千只

没有翅膀的蜜蜂　　　　　在原地摇晃　不再

生产　　　　　　产品　　不再　　考虑

清楚　酒醉的条纹　　　碰撞　电视机上的人物

像浮木　　　摩擦　　　婴儿的头　　转

向他们　　　形状已经　　脱　　离

他们的　　　身体　一切　都在漂浮　房子的

框架　　不见了　　所剩下的垂下　　像一件

衬衫　　母亲们坐在下面　缝水　这儿

书页　　　　在翻动但没有人　　在读　这儿

我们　　　没有才华　　这儿　我们　　　　　暴雨一般

婴儿总在长大　　　　　这儿一盏灯　在一座

房子里　　　在一条街上继续闪烁　　　　在痛苦之中

*

如果都说　　　　　幸福是　　水　　　　　　并且

一直在　　　成长　　　那么像我这样的　　　一定是

月面火山口的那种　　　　形状是环形的吝啬于　　　流动

有时候我不能　　控制它的　　脱去它的　　叛逆

还有时候　　它突然冻结而我凿啊　　凿　　用一把

冰锥　　直到我的手指　　　冻成了一颗　　洋蓟

一名推着婴儿车的男子说　　　这值得　　但是　感觉

像　　蹄子踏在我脸上　　我　不能　　仰卧推举它

我想要一个　　固定收入的你　　　这样　　我会告诉你　　我不

想　　　你留下　　我想　　　　叫醒　　每一个

早晨　还有　　找到　　布制的你　在我　　　　　身边

我想要　　　　戳你　还要　　挠　　你　　我想要

成为　　你的裤管内缝长度　去为你剪裁　去　　穿上

你　去　　成为　　　　你

*

如果你是　　双孢蘑菇　　那我们就是　双孢蘑菇

的　　底部　　　　　是嵌入的嘴唇　　　　即使

欲望也会　　被分割　　　　　　百叶窗　　切割

我们的脸　切成　　　丰富　　　每天　我们

被　　重新切割　每天我们尝试　　去推动我们的

自我　重新推到一起　　　像青草　　　每一个　夜晚

引爆　　　　试图将自己　贴上　早晨的　　　　光

每天　我们　被重新命名就像一个　　　新的　　雨季

我们被推着向前划水　　　一次　又　　一次　　盐水

被滴水击中　每一次　　　冲击　都不同　　　　　　于

下一次　　　这儿　我们　　　病了但 没有 任何

症状　　　这儿的　　雨　　总是　挤得水泄不通

这儿我们　永远　　　穿　露　背

长袍　但是　不知　为何

*

一位老者　　推起　一棵菩提树的　　　锁骨

只有　烟灰知道为什么　　会　　从他的烟头

掉落　像星号般　　他没有抬头看　　　我们的身体

和　　　婴儿车重叠　新铺的水泥蒸腾　　着

灰泥房子和　新的表皮　　婴儿的脸　　映在

店面上　　我们的皮肤　像　　仙人掌　　　我们

与　　这片　风景　紧紧相连　　这儿的树　　需要

木头棍子　　才能挺直　　腰板　这儿的工人们修剪

蓟草　　　在小道上　　每天工作　　一路

向西　然后　回来　这儿的田野　被冲了气　　成了

中国跳棋的棋盘　　坨坨　　　黄土散落

像　　五彩纸屑好像有什么要　　庆祝　这儿

我们试着去摆脱　　废墟　趁着白天　　但当夜幕降临

我们的　　　双手　总是荒芜一片

*

我是内翻足　　　　朝内扭曲　　外翻　向下　我是

千分　之一　的　　沙尘暴　　　一名男子

说你应该感到　　　　　　幸福　看看　你自己的

孩子　但如果　　幸福　就在　孩子　身上

那幸福就会　　　跑　　掉　　爬上　阶梯

穿过蓝色的　隧道　滑下　　　滑梯

我要　　　笔直　　不弯曲　　我追赶我的

另一只脚就像　　追彩票　我仔细分析要成为那千万分之一的

中奖者　给我的强力球以力量　　　我百万的

百万　　我阶乘的　能力　　　算上风的

因素　还有　窗户　以及下雨的　　　　　可能性

我奖金所剩下的 　　　　就只有这个 　我想回

家 　就现在 　　我想要自己的房间 　永远这样 　我要

我曾 　拥有的 　　　　我要 　　　我现在拥有的

*

最后一座城市的 　　　最后一个停车场 　有

一棵棵树 　看起来 　　像神经末梢 　头皮般的 　　树叶

千万只鸟 　三只一队 　某个地方 　有那么

最后一群人 　已经 　停了下来 　把 　白色的石头放到

干涸的火山上 　贝丝喜欢 　吉姆 　　　有人喜欢

马特 　在最后的聚会上 　灯 　光 　长矛般穿过人群

照到最后一个婴儿的 　　脸上 　小小的身体 　深深 　陷在

无知之中 　有一次教一个 　　孩子怎样 　　画

一个人　　　我知道了我们就是由　　　圆形和

矩形组成　　我现在知道　身体要　　　先放松

才能收紧　　我现在知道身体　　能放松　　　还能

和很多男子　一起收紧　　我现在知道　地球　是一个

洞　　而不是一个　球体　　　　要用　身体

来装　　　满　　而不是　　　用思想

*

圆形的锯子　锯着软骨　　　　　　收紧时间

我在想　　时间　是不是　　　在逃　避

死亡　还是在走向死亡　我　　在想　　　死

听起来　　是不是　　这样的　　　还是死　　　并

没有声音　　餐车　　按响　　　喇叭　那

太阳推　　　啊　　推着　　　　九位　推着婴儿车的

母亲　婴儿坐得　　笔直像风筝　　　　一名女子的

雕像上有一个　　　位置　是心　该有的　　　位置

穿过空间　　在公园的　　　　另一头　　　有

一面美国国旗　　这个雕像　一定是一名男子　　做的

我们总是把女子们　　　　　看成　　　透明　男子们

快要完成砌墙的　工作　　　　　　一块石头　　接着

一块石头　我们把　　嘴唇　上的　奶　滴

擦去　给　树梢　带去　　　快乐

*

昨天我有了自己的　　　　　房间和　　我自己的

马利筋但我不　　　想　待在　那里

52

楼下一个婴儿　　　第一次　　　在地板上

滚动　像黎明一般　　　　她笑了　　　拍手

然后她哭着　　　滚到了　　　沙发上　　　获得

主动权的她　失去了主动权　　　我梦到　　　　　　我

终于可以　　　　离开这个家　　　但我得

穿过　　　一条满是蜜蜂的小巷　　　　　小巷

有六英尺宽　　　蜜蜂有六英寸　　　长　　　　它们

在我的脊背上　　　嗡嗡作响　　把我引向北方引到一座镇上

那里的每个人都在靠近苹果树的地方　　　工作　那里没有人

制作旗帜　　那里　每个人都学着如何把沉默

翻倍　如何把　　　悲伤　切成　小　　　块

如何　　　收集　　　颜色送给　　　别人

*

每个人都希望　　　诗里　有一个皇帝　一颗头颅

被绳子一圈圈　　　套住　但这首　　　诗不够热情　这首

诗不是史诗　小道　　　　灌木丛　　　一名男子坐在

拖拉机上　　在地里　　挖坑　就好像　　　那

地　　就是　地　　而不是　　　血肉　一个　接着

一个　虫子像小　　豆子一样　　从　　草丛里

被扯了出来　　　没有　　　　别的方法　它们

成千上万　　被踢到了　它们就缩成　　　小球

虫身　像泥土一样滚动　　　　它们没有声音

但我们无法　　抹去它们的尖叫　一个怪诞的

故事但不是什么　大不了的故事　　　即使在这里　也有战争

54

有一台金属机器　　　有　　　一项毫无意义的　　　工作

有恐怖　　　我们的　　　漠视和　　　数十亿　　　的

身体蜂拥　　　而出　　　　　　　像被烟熏过的　　　蜜蜂

*

我们又一次无视　　　星球的存在　　　　　冥王星　　　不

再是举手表决时　　　　　还能算得上的星球了　　　身体

都到　　哪里去了如果　　　所有的手　　都上了甲板　当

手回来时怎样　　　才能找到　　　　　身体

大地上的　　　人　　花　　　　　　　一年时间

吟唱　手啊手　　　手指拇指嘀嘀嗒嗒

嘀嘀嗒嗒　　嗒嗒嗒　　　　　　与鲨鱼不同　我们

狩猎不是　　通过　　倾听　彼此的　　　心声

我们狩猎　　靠的是我们的　　　　双手　我们的手

总是　在　　一个轮子后面在一条路上　路把

松树　分成　不同的部落　　　　在周六　　　某人的

手会　在　　另一个　　　人的脖子上　拉紧

绳索　　　我们　　　会　　用我们的手　写下一切

无论怎样　手都不会像心一样　　　被包住

*

雨　　被天空　脱去衣裳　　　土壤

敞开怀抱　接纳了　　雨　就好像　　它有

答案　因为土壤　　　没有任何　　选择

因为　土壤也　　受到攻击　　那里　有

钻石　在　　土壤的　　森林　　深处

上帝　的　　脓包　　　　如果你把　　　　钻石

用高温　　加热　它　会　　像　女子　一样

消失　　　在　空　气　里　　　　有钻石

在婴儿的脚　和剪下的　　柔软的　　指甲下面

这儿　　　雨　　没有　　　嘴巴　与其

说是舌头　不如说是一巴掌　　卡片上写着祝贺

用手帮我冲洗　　　你　小小的嘴巴　　说着

给了我　　一个吻　　　　雨滴　把　我的脸

映照　成了　　　千万　个　你的脸

*

如果黑暗　可以被　　梳理那　　　就会有

数百个　　结　早晨和　　夜晚

交错　在　　水泥地上　　　　　　一只蜗牛　　　被压扁

成　　尖叫的　　　形状　一条鱼　　　从　　水中

挣脱出来　　它　　鱼竿般的身体　　　是泥土上

闪烁的光　　行走的人　　　踩过　　　　鱼的眼睛

某个地方有个孩子　抽打着　　　　　　身体

试图　醒来　　　　某个地方的虫子　　抓着　恶棍般的

泥土　蠕虫　　　在死后　　　看起来　　　更

漂亮　　只蜜蜂　　夹在了一辆　　婴儿车的轮子里

发出噼啪声　就好像　　　它的心可以被压碎　如果我们

向前　推　　轮子　我们　无视　　　　死亡如果

我们向后退　我们就重复　死亡　所以我们

站着　不动　　　　试图　超越　死亡

*

两块真人大小的油布　　　雪人　用绳子　　　固

定住　光像血液一样流淌在草坪上　　　鹿的

头移动着　带着小小的角　　　看　　他

在梯子上　　爬　　上　　爬下　　　一把梯子

不同的　　开始和结束　底下　能

听到　蠕虫正在　　从　　土壤里　　钻出来

上面看得到　月亮　底部　的

灰尘　那是灰尘　　也是　婚姻　的

隐喻　　　我厌恶草坪　厌恶雪人　　还有

那胡萝卜鼻子　　恶心的微笑　大自然的　　尽头但

我什么都不懂　　婴儿看到　　光芒　看到

雪人　笑了　我怎样才能解释复活节的由来　　　然后

我们画彩蛋　我们把彩蛋藏起来　我们找到彩蛋

我们在它们上面　　　撒上盐　　　我们把它们　吃了

*

蜘蛛每天的　工作　不是　创造　美

而是进食　　人的思维　　　　　与心灵

脱离　保持完美的　　　　距离　因为

距离　我们不可能　把一切　　　都看成美

我们　和　　　蜘蛛　的　　区别　是　　我们

可以　让　　事物活下去　草坪上的出售告示

阴影升起　　但　　我们走后　阴影又下沉　夏天

损伤了　　放牛肉干的　空袋子　　　擦去了

某人清单的　　　　一半　在水沟旁　剩下的

是什么　　棕色的　　赭色的小屋　神秘的是

清单似乎　摆放得　　如此　用

心　就像　在　路旁

摆上　一束丁香花　而　我们　知道

花朵　并　不能　代表　美

*

我　又在思考　幸福是什么　想到

你在某种　　别样的正字法中　也许你

是　盲文的凸起　或许是你的存在

让　我得以　　审视　低压区

那经常带来　雨水的部分　没有　掌声

没有　低语　你是　我　　把　　回声

看成　悲痛　之外的事物的原因　光芒在这儿但

只是一种　　补充　太阳不过是　光的

一种来源　光　　不过是　　　肉眼　可察觉的

波长　光不是　　幸福　我追寻你的

底部　那苔藓般　满是毛囊的暗面　　光囊括了

一切　被完美地　装订好　　因为完美的

黑暗是不可能　　创造出来的　我追寻它就像一只眼睛

追寻　另一只眼睛的　　黑色的　　　洞

*

又一个　　　早晨　终于　有名男子　被雇来

把砾石板　铺在　土路上就好像　　泥土也

需要　被　　驯服　另一名男子在　　　快

走　甩着　胳膊　　　他　挂绳上的

照片褪色了　他的双眼　　在休战　　有一名消瘦的女子

她没有　　面孔　因为跑　　马拉松　　　面无表情

她的　身体记得　　疼痛　和　　记得　痛苦的

方式　不同　　　疼痛是　　　一串

珍珠　痛苦是　　珍珠散落　她走过　　躺在婴儿车里的

婴儿身旁　男婴想要够到　　脚趾　他在练习　如何

去抓　一个　女孩子　　一个女孩子　能跑多远

跑进　森林　一个女孩子可以　　跑　一半的路

跑进　森林　从那之后　她就　　一直想

跑　出　森林

*

如果男人是　土地　那女人就是　放在　土地上的

烧杯　　　　放在　一堆　其他　烧杯　上面

放在　学校的　　　柜子里　　　如果

女人　是　烧杯　那　婴儿就是　表面

皿　平整地　　盖住她　　但　并不

完全　　　把她封死　还可以　　　交换气体

如果婴儿是　　　表面皿　　那么　诗歌就是

月亮　试图　　　倾斜　它的光芒

透过　　　表面皿　变成　一束　不可分割的

眩光　　　像一串　流苏　慢慢垂下

越过　表面皿　留下　　　液滴

64

像　　灌木上的霜　一样　　　　　　　绽放

让底部　　　一切　　　都　　绽开　在

一片　白色的　　　火光之中

*

野心　奔跑的　　　终点是　　　一块

硬邦邦的　　白面包　　　未被刀切　　放在一张木桌上

我还是想切　这块面包　　想吃面包但是

已经　太晚了　　我还是想　　摇晃　撒盐罐

那形状像个怀孕的　雪人　那被毁容的

变得坚硬的　简单的　　雪人的眼睛不是　　一扇

窗户　它们是胎死腹中的　纸　　这儿　没有

希腊诸神　　只有　婴儿　尖锐的哭啼声　　　还有

她出生的　　个人传说　　这儿　成功并不是

有一尊　　　你的蜡像　　黏稠的痰液　皮屑

一个个吻变成了　　疹子　红疹爬满　　手腕

在野心的　　尽头有　　雪　　形状　像

要送人的　　信仰骰子　一切的终极

充满阳刚之气　　和一小瓶　　又一小瓶的　　欢乐

三

去年的词语属于
去年的语言。

明年的词语等待
另一个声音。

——T.S.艾略特《四个四重奏》

友谊——于 2015 年 8 月 3 日之后慢慢死去。父亲的朋友们来看他。他们坐在椅子上说中文。把词典当衣服穿。配偶间的眼神很奇怪。朋友们回家后感觉良好，因为他们尽了责任，拾起了零碎的文字。每个人都回忆起了共事的时光，回忆起看到太阳另一边的情景。朋友们来的次数越来越少。他们自己也被死亡追赶。我想到叶子以及它们和果实的关系。叶子关心膨胀的果实吗？果实膨胀的时候有考虑过叶子吗？也许叶子会在果实生长的时候为它遮阳，果实会为叶子散发香气。但最终各自都必须独立面对自己的坠落。

护工——于 2009 年、2010 年、2011 年、2012 年、2013 年、2014 年、2015 年、2016 年、2017 年一个个相继死去。有个没来，因为她的丈夫被捕。大多数其他人都在看时间等下班。时间终究会为活着的人停歇，我们由此可以走出大门。时间之门的把手对垂死的人来说太烫手。如果无法走出，那大门还有什么用？无法打开的大门叫做墙。在另一边，玻璃会绽放。父亲就在墙的另一边。另一边的西红柿快熟了。我可以透过同样打不开的窗户看到。无法打开的窗户就是透明的墙。有时候，我们坐在里面，就像在飞机上。大多数时候，我们从外面往里看，就像在狗狗托儿所。我不知道西红柿是不是他语言的新形式，还是只是用来食用。我问不了他，因为在另一边没有词语。我所能做的就是盯着这些无名的、爆裂的西红柿，知道这已足够。

主题——总是死去，留给我们的是一间变暗的房间里的建筑、形式、声音，还有几把没摆好的椅子。门被反锁了。尽管如此，主题还是闯了进来，所有的事物都站了起来。母亲的死不是她的故事。父亲中风也不是他的故事。我不是母亲的故事，也不是父亲的。但有一个隐蔽的交汇点，那里有所有走向冷漠的地图。痛苦能和主题分离吗？主题能飞翔、迷失方向、在另一棵树上啄食吗？怎样才能背负沉重的主题前行而不践踏所有的草坪呢？

悲伤——死的时候，街对面的人正在修剪灌木丛，而我能看到我的孩子们在翻筋斗。或者在那一刻，我正静静地坐着倾听天空的声音，思量着直升机或是孩子晚上嘶哑的呼吸声。死后的时间改变了形状，微微向下滚落，就好像无需我们的帮助也能自己向前移动。因为死后并没有所谓的"放手前行"，尽管有人在破碎的灯光下向我们招手。只有一把石钥匙可以插入一把石锁。但是死去的人拿着钥匙。而石头是溪流中的巨石。我招来回忆，用一把木勺敲打，就那么一瞬，让时间停止无意义的欢闹，就那么一瞬，再次感受死亡的箔片，那肮脏血腥的喙。

共情——在 2017 年 1 月 20 日之前的某个时刻死了。大门消失了，而我们却不知道是在什么时候。门铃消失。火车停运。有人偷了"北极"的标志。我是你，是你，还有你。但横在我们中间的有太多的障碍。我永远无法感受到母亲的病痛或是父亲的痴呆。乐谱上的黑色音符只代表了声音，琴键必须敲击特定的琴弦，而琴弦是由钢丝制成的，而钢丝是由地下得来的铁和碳冶炼而成。我们为什么要制造钢琴这样的事物来表现美和痛？我们为什么要画下看到的事物？谈到绘画，母亲常说："临摹就行。"艺术家只是探访了痛并去想象它。我们赞美的是艺术家，而不是苹果，也不是正被慢慢谋杀的苹果的影子。一定有某种作画的方式，让画不至于成为一首挽歌。

讣告作者——可能比讣告的对象先死。约翰·威尔逊死于 2002 年，在他发表乐队领队亚提·萧的讣告之前，而后者死于 2004 年。要是我比父亲先死呢？自从他中风后，我每天都在脑海中写他的讣告。父亲的大脑比他先死。大脑被心爱的头骨包围着。要是他头骨的铰链断裂，脑子掉了出来呢？是还给他还是扔掉？要是我们叫服务生，来的却是上帝呢？我们是让个座给上帝一杯白兰地，还是遮住双眼希望上帝看不到自己？母亲多年来一直知道自己会死。但在最后的日子里，她却一脸茫然。为此，心知肚明地遭了那么久的罪，却在最后不能给已知的事情画上句号。我为什么要在她最后的时刻再去告诉她？像奥克兰仓库大火中丧生的人，匍匐在地上，想要分清一个损坏的器官和一扇门，分清一座楼梯和一片阴影。死亡不是敌人，知道死亡才是。

你看到这棵树了吗？

它的秘密像柠檬一样生长。

有时，我假装

爱我的孩子们胜过

爱词语——除了词语，谁都不知道。

*

孩子们啊，我的孩子们，

今天，我的手一碰到

你们的头发就开始做梦。

你们的头发变成了冬天。

我死的时候，你们的头发会下雪。

医生——死于 2015 年 8 月 3 日，被之前所有的医生围着，他们的眼睛本应该泛红，却没有。俄裔的医生比谁都更早知道死亡将至，先提到了"安宁医疗"这个词，乍一看以为就是"安宁"和"医疗"。是其中哪个词？渴望一个人尽快死去似乎是错误的。去医院餐厅抱着一桌的吐司、果酱、发亮的黄油似乎是错误的。想要延长遭受痛苦之人的生命似乎是错误的。我们想要兰花，还是游弋在湖中央的天鹅？我们能触摸兰花，而它不会动。兰花是我们所理解的死亡，但天鹅才是死亡。

昨天——死于午夜时分。全身金黄。手帕因为悲痛而湿润。约翰·厄普代克曾说过："每天醒来，我们都稍微有所不同，昨天的我们已经死了。既然死亡无时无刻不在，那为什么还要害怕死亡？"厄普代克一定没有亲眼目睹过一个人慢慢窒息而死。空气像丝绸一样在我们肺的褶皱里进进出出。但呼吸是一场幸运的意外。厄普代克一定没有见过死神端来一杯杯水却不说话。他一定从未在时间流血的时候把它扛在肩膀上。我想现在经历过死亡的他一定会改变看法。他吐出的话可能不再是小鸟，而是绷带。似乎只有活着的人才会假设死亡，才会试着把死亡扶起来。

悲痛——我所认识的悲痛已经死了很多次了。悲痛死的时候正要和别的更轻微的死亡重逢。每天早晨，我铺开孩子们的衣裳来遮住她们的悲痛。悲痛仍在，却被覆盖的事物改变。遗忘的照片不等同于遗忘。我的悲痛也不等同于我的疼痛。我的母亲是位数学家，所以我试着去计算我的悲痛。我的父亲是位工程师，所以我试着在悲痛周围做一个盒子，盒子里有一张小木床，悲痛可以躺在上面。文字不停地打断我的悲痛，迫使我说些无意义的话。如果你剪下一片蓝得完美的矩形天空，没有云，没有风，没有鸟，用一个蓝色的框子把它裱上，面朝上，放在一个空无一物的博物馆的地板上，博物馆的中庭向天空敞开，这就是悲痛。

医生 —— 死于 2014 年 7 月 16 日。
林奇医生应该是最好的。我调查过。
我打过电话。我问过。我读到过。我
受过的所有的教育让我做好准备来帮
助母亲。我是死神孩子中书读得最
多、最年幼的一个。候诊室里的上百
号人都拿着绿色的氧气瓶。周围的空
气是我一个人的，我却无法呼吸。我
们等了两个小时。医生穿着一件银
行家标配的蓝色衬衫，丝滑的红色
领带遮住了他的肺。母亲指着我说：
"我想活得长一点，这样我就有更多
时间来陪她。"我觉得她指的是我所
代表的我的孩子们。医生把 X 光片
夹在小灯箱上。他的笔指着所有多
出来的黑点。他说话的时候，我应
该有所感觉。我把头转了过去，因
为我从来没有看到过母亲的内脏器
官。这样去看的方式是错误的。我
现在知道小时候被爱是被看护。在
高中，我喜欢老师把灯关掉的一刻，
这一刻我感受到自己被爱着，同时
又不被看到。我现在明白了。关灯
的时候，我们不可能被爱。

责怪——想死却死不了。它的头发乱蓬蓬，但它一直都在。母亲责怪父亲。我责怪父亲的痴呆。父亲责怪母亲不运动。父亲是故事，不是讲故事的人。我最终责怪了父亲，因为故事总想成为讲故事的人。责怪是没有面孔的。我在它的楼梯上走了一圈又一圈，想给它一巴掌，但打到的却是自己的脸颊。有些人受苦了，就想把自己的苦告诉所有人。梳子梳到了一个结，孩子就会放声大哭，发出一种表达痛苦的声音，但这不是痛苦本身。我的想象力不能让我感受到孩子的痛苦，能感受到的只是痛苦的回音。责怪只是痛苦的回音，是你所责怪之人脸上的一层面纱。我责怪上帝。我想向上帝的老板投诉上帝。要是上帝的老板是雨，要是与雨对话的唯一方式是向天空张开你的嘴巴然后淹死呢？

时间——死于 2015 年 8 月 3 日。母亲死前一周，护士打来电话说："做好心理准备吧。"我翻了翻包，想找到剩下的词语。我的口袋里空空如也。准备好什么？没有词语，我还能准备吗？带着花蕾的茎是花朵吗？花蕾不是花朵，而是即将绽放的花朵。除了"垂死"，没有别的词可以形容"即将死亡"，但即使是垂死也缺少时间，和花蕾缺少时间轴一样。母亲以为只是感染。她责怪医生没有早点给她用抗生素，这是她说过的最后一句让人听得明白的话。但时间已经走在了她的前面，车轮已经开始转动。护士事后说："我很惊讶她能撑过周末。"我很惊讶她竟然死了。时间不是一瞬间。时间被放大，变得模糊。就像我十岁的女儿为自己的生日把我死去的母亲的手镯包了起来，说那是给她的礼物。

今天，我向你们展示
住在帐篷里的人。
如果你凑过来
仔细听，柠檬会发出声响，
捶捶拳头，就会掉下来。

*

孩子们啊，我的孩子们，
你们知道一颗死去的心会鸣响吗？
我的呼吸是一幅
你们不会忘记的画面，
你们会把它像床单一样掀开。

形式——死于 2015 年 8 月 3 日。母亲死后，天气就逐渐热了起来，而我们则都成了盲人。又有一只鸟从榕树上掉了下来，留下了它的蛋。转动大地的手臂从未为鸟儿停留过，而鸟儿则被碾碎在大地与时间之间。母亲死后，我对她的爱完全失去了形状。我对她的一切厌恶都变得纤维化。我让一切变硬、窒息。我在网上的肺纤维化论坛上发帖讲述她最后的日子，对着陌生人打字到深夜，我们的指尖触碰到了一起。故事还在那儿，但我再也找不到了，也找不到那些或许已经死去的人。每一条讯息都是一名小士兵，排成队列，供新的垂死之人阅读，看看当他们失去知觉后，活着的人会如何看待他们。悲痛不是从破口的鸡蛋中溢出的事物。悲痛是一排在冷风中失去队形的鸡蛋。

控制——和母亲一起死于 2015 年 8 月 3 日。突然间，我不再身处大地的中央。突然间，我可以调整水笔的角度，让火箭朝另一个方向飞。所有的孩子都停止了哭泣。我姐姐约了神经科医生。医生问道："你叫什么名字？"父亲回答："什么系统是什么……什么。"他把手伸进钱包，把信用卡递给了医生。他的手指愤怒地指着我。我们拿了给父亲的处方——抗抑郁药、抗焦虑药、愤怒管理的药。母亲没想过给他用药。很多事情都取决于我们怎么问问题。"他感觉如何？"与"你感觉如何？"有着天壤之别。我紧紧抓住那张小纸片，它在风中缓缓地飘动，像是一面投降的旗帜。那天，黄昏没有到来。我走了进去。

情况 —— 至少是部分情况，死于
2015 年 8 月 3 日，而父亲则是另一
种情况。情况不像一件你可以随时
从别人身上脱去的夹克。情况是皮
肤，是身体的蛋壳，是花盆。你把
时钟的指针拿掉，时钟还在。时间
继续，因为指针代表时间，但不是
时间本身。想让情况死去但留下人，
就像要骑马飞驰但不要马一样。有
很多事物我无法用一个盒子来装：
风、奇迹、时间、苦难。我没有答
案。我没有别的问题。因为"什么
时候？"就意味着情况会结束。我的
脸上浮现着两位死者的面容。而我
终于可以放下词典了。

记忆 ——死于 2015 年 2 月 12 日。和往常一样。我们到了，孩子们给母亲一个拥抱，然后离开房间去看电视。我则会坐在离我送给她的乐至宝牌椅子十英尺远的小凳子上。氧气机疲惫不堪，发出汩汩的声响，父亲在另一个房间踱步。母亲说："阿里巴巴。"我问："什么？"她重复道："是阿里巴巴，我想买些股。"之后几周，母亲一遍遍地问我，就好像还是头一次问。我还能听见她的声音，带着口音的"阿""里"和"巴巴"的尖声合唱，最后两个字跟中文里的爸爸相似。甚至在临死的时候，她还认为通向上帝的道路是金钱。我在想她在梦里会不会听到硬币的声音，上帝抚摸她额头的时候，上帝的指尖是不是感觉像是黄金。我在三月给她买了阿里巴巴的股票，现在已经涨了 40.64%。

医生——死于 2015 年 8 月 3 日。林奇医生、张医生、马奥尼医生、急诊室的医生、护士，他们都面无表情地把薄薄的毯子拉到母亲的肩头，冰冷的夏天。马奥尼医生终于来了，我却忘记了所有要问的问题。我的心像伞一样打开。他说要离开诊所。我在想为什么要称医生团队叫"诊所"，就好像他们还不是能确诊的专家。也许是因为他们只有自己死了才知道怎样去死。他说话的时候，我尽量不散发温暖的气息。他想试试"别的疗法"，就好像拯救我的母亲也可以是一种职业选择。他说了二十分钟。我们忘记了她还躺在小床上，和三名痛苦呻吟的女士就隔着一道帘子。我们就这样来来回回地关心他人。回到母亲房间的时候，我滑下显微镜，感到自己在不断缩小。

痴迷 ——生于 1940 年 1 月 20 日，在中风后从未死去，反而继续成长。中风得到了一扇橡木门，不仅坚实，还密不透风。痴迷的事物在橡木门后孤独地生活。中风后，痴迷带着父亲去了健身房在跑步机上散步。他散起步来像是穿越一场野火，他走啊走，走得不见了。现在，他的大脑有了口音，谁都不知道该如何阻止他学习这种新的语言。母亲来电说他摔在了跑步机上，撞破了头，抗凝剂像月光一样播洒他的血液。他的头被钻了孔，血液和更多的词语被抽了出来。父亲终于被捕，他交出了剩下的词语，舌头被绑了起来。他在白纸上做着梦。

孩子们啊，我的孩子们，
今晚的朗诵会上，
一位白人作家说：
"她是个眯眼的婊子。"
我的"眯眯眼"没有睁开。

*

我的孩子们没有
"眯眯眼"，有的是呼吸。
呼吸把道路送入
白人男子的体内。
这样的道路通椋鸟。

时钟 —— 死于 2009 年 6 月 24 日，死得不是时候。多少次父亲没有通过画钟测试。有一次，我在收音机里听到一位患有老年痴呆症的科学家想找出他画不了时钟的原因。这和"三种类型的叠加"有关。时针上的 1 到 12 代表了小时；分针上的 1 不代表 1 分钟而是 5 分钟，2 代表了 10 分钟；然后还有秒针，从 1 到 60。我停在红绿灯前想着时钟，想着它完美的圆和"叠加"，想着一个平面上所有复杂的层次。然而，健康人却能不假思索地在一瞬间读出时间。我想到父亲和他所缺失的不假思索，他的思绪都是第二、第三、第四次思考，无法找回最重要的第一次。我想到收音机里的那个人，他的大脑现在又退化到了什么程度。我惊讶于我们的大脑允许语言漫无目的地游走而不用回头看，却知道码头在哪里。如果你拆开一只纸折天鹅并把纸张压平，纸张会因为看到过天鹅的形状而悲伤吗？还是它向往平整、没有褶皱的生活？父亲就是那张纸。他记得天鹅却叫不出名字。他不再记得纸上的天鹅代表了活生生的天鹅。他的大脑是活生生的天鹅曾游弋过的湖水，容纳了一切，但冰融化的时候，所有的鱼都消失了。我们说的所有的词大多和鱼有关。走了，就一去不复返。

希望——死于 2014 年 10 月 15 日。当天，美国药监局批准了治疗肺纤维化的两种药，吡非尼酮和尼达尼布。我把所学过的都用上了，做了研究阅读，提出了问题。我把论文都贴到墙上，现在看起来像是墓碑。希望是最狂野的鸟，它飞得太快，要么消失，要么化作烈焰。我从日本带回来的咖啡杯上写着"享受幸福时光"这几个字。就好像知道幸福和时间有着某种联系。药物可以减缓病情，但无法逆转。我们选择了安宁疗护。我孩子的家庭作业上有这么一道题："以下哪种情况最终会发生？ a. 你出生了，b. 你死了，c. 漫长的冬天结束了，d. 熟能生巧。"我已经不知道该如何回答了。

头颅——死于 2015 年 8 月 3 日。两名男子终于来了，他们把轮床推到另一个房间，轻声的交谈和不多的噪音，然后轮床的一端就像游轮一样驶了出来。他们担心会撞到墙壁。母亲的全身盖着一条毯子。她的头不见了。她的脸不见了。里尔克错了。没有了头，身体什么都不是。现在被盖住的母亲已经不再是我的母亲了。被遮住的苹果不再是苹果。一个人的素描不是那个人。那天早晨，不知在哪里，母亲变成了素描。而我则会用余生把她再描回来。

蓝色的连衣裙——悄无声息地和小蓝花一起死于 2015 年 8 月 6 日。花瓣曾抬头绽放。现在则成了片片尘埃。我在想有没有烧连衣裙，还是只是烧了遗体？我在想是谁把她托起，放入大火之中？我在想她的头发在变成篝火前有没有拂过她的脸庞？我在想身体燃烧时会发出什么声音？葬礼上，她的头发被染了，染得太黑了。她看起来像是个漫画人物。我等待着下一个漫画框，等待着去读对话气泡，看她会说什么。但没有等来她的话，有的只是吹完玻璃后的静谧。雨不可逆转。还有数百万朵小蓝花。想象力是指不得不活在死者的未来。悲痛永远穿着死者的连衣裙。

后知后觉——在 2015 年 8 月 3 日之前从未存在过。有人把后知后觉涂掉了。但如果你涂掉了什么，那它仍然存在。在某些夜晚，孩子们刷牙的时候，我会躲到她们的被子底下，等她们回房间，我就会跳出来。我尽量让自己躺平，尽量不动，就好像我已经死了。每次我都气喘吁吁。每次我都意识到我不想死。每次我都意识到死亡并不在乎我想要什么。有时候，有一个孩子会尖叫，但大多数时候，她们会看出我的形状或是看到我的脚，知道我还活着。我真希望事先就能知道母亲死亡的确切时间。就像预约一样。那样的话，我就会更早地调动我的情感。我就不会涂掉她的嘴。我就不会涂掉我的心。现在一切都结束了。我知道心并没有真的碎掉，但我再也感觉不到它了。

牧师——死于 2015 年 8 月 3 日。临死的时候，他骂了粗口。这位牧师刚来我们家的时候会在门上留下水印。没过多久，母亲的门上就满是他拳头子弹般的印记。他开始用眼神向我传送祈祷。我不需要他的祈祷。我有太多的自我，上帝是无法拯救的。没有一个自我知道如何说对不起。没有一个自我认识彼此。我在想，母亲临终的时候有没有接受上帝？就像她每天早上都会悉心照料她的五十盆盆景，轻轻地给它们修剪枝叶，调整小型喷头，用她的呼吸召唤它们。盆景几乎从不回应，也从未要求受到限制。她说牧师很"奇怪"，还会用诡异的眼神看她。就好像他知道她不是信徒，而是难民。她刚来这个国家的时候，她的皮肤被涂掉了。她患灰指甲的脚趾看起来像树根。

我穿上一件衬衫，
套上一条工作裤，
因为我会死。
雪是如何掉落至死的，
雪是如何装扮成雨的。

*

在哪里能找到希望？
有时候，城市有褶皱，
有时候，身体
响起紫罗兰般的喜悦，
有时候，夜晚的风凉飕飕。

汽车——很难带走，死于 2015 年 3 月 13 日。母亲死前，父亲为驾照考试复习了半年，就好像那是通往天堂的入学考试。母亲给他找来中文的旧考题。他坐在桌前，手托着头，喃喃自语，一遍遍走到母亲的椅子前，他身下汇成了一条小河。"2. 上帝突然插到你前面造成危险。你应该先采取以下哪种措施？ a. 按喇叭并用力踩刹车，b. 松开油门，c. 快速换到旁边的车道。"还有选项 d 吗？"加速，碾过上帝。"

我母亲最喜欢的盆栽——死于2016年，死得很慢。那天，我抬起头，看到粉红色的花朵不见了，树枝成了破败的鸦片枪，只有那花盆还认得出来。我把盆栽移植到我这儿，它还是死了。我的邻居坚持说它还活着，就好像坚持就能让它重新开花。他的父母还活着，所以我就由他这么说。有天早晨，花盆里出现了黑色的小喷头。我已忘记了别人的希望。我已忘记了别人。我只剩下一个朋友——死神。那年，我辞去了工作。我给孩子们梳头的时候，小鸟从头发下面飞了出来。母亲一定会有意见的。我看得到她的脸，因为我没把故事讲对。随着时间的流逝，我对她的记忆就像一头夜行的野兽在屋顶上飞奔。我知道那是头野兽，但我永远无法看到它，也不知道它什么时候还会来。

明喻——死于 2015 年 8 月 3 日。除
了死亡本身，没有什么像死亡。没
有什么像悲痛，除了悲痛本身。就
像铁丝网的影子看起来像鱼的鳞片
却永远都不是。有次母亲很晚来电
说她便秘。街灯看起来像是长长的
拱形手臂。黑暗中，我坐在她的床
边。浴室里的微光还跟一切别无二
致。塑料坐浴看起来像是什么，我
把它装满水又倒掉。她的两只胳膊
还能在膝盖上压小碗。我就跟她说
了该怎么做。要是词语表达思想能
像麦克风表达词语一样就好了。

亲情——死于 1978 年 11 月 12 日，我看到的最后一张母亲搂着我的照片。在葬礼上，我没有伸手去碰我姐姐。散场时，她和配偶坐在第一排。我看到他的手臂在她肩膀上抬起又落下。我配偶的父母去世时，他两次都泪流满面，收不住的泪水也很快被收住。第一次，他拥抱的人是我，而不是他的家人。第二次，他谁都没有拥抱。护士来电说："很抱歉，你母亲今天早晨去世了。"我把这个消息告诉了孩子们，我们三个人抱成一团，眼泪夺眶而出。就好像眼泪本来就在那儿自己哭着，而被夺去亲人的我们破眶而出。从眼泪中走回来的第一人称的我每次都会丧失更多的一点自我。

家——大约在 1960 年母亲离开台北时死去了。家又死于 2015 年 8 月 3 日。家的指尖每次都被削平。新的残肢有了意识，成了统领，就是矮了一截、胖了一点。家现在是一面叫做玫瑰山纪念公园的镜子。从北京到台北到纽约到宾夕法尼亚到密歇根到加利福尼亚到玫瑰山，不知她走了多远。有白人作家让一个小说人物叫另一个"眯眯眼的婊子"，我就寻找母亲。我叫她的名字，但想不起她的声音。我觉得是有点眯眯眼。她会说："别听老美的，我们最终都会到一个地方去。"但这个地方在哪里呢？那儿有门吗？有猫尾草吗？现在她的喉咙里满是铁丝网，她的话胎死腹中。自从我上次来过之后，所有平躺在地上的新墓碑，就像草坪上的小担架。我躺在她的墓碑旁闭上双眼。我现在知道了很多事情。即使闭着眼睛，我也知道一只小鸟从我头顶上飞过。在上吊小人的游戏中，身体在被吊起的过程中形成。就像我们在死亡中成长。

当一位母亲死去，

一座房子就变成了一座森林。

孩子们啊，我的孩子们，

我就在树上。

真爱意味着你们找不到我。

*

孩子们啊，我的孩子们，

记得要放手让我走，

删除我的号码，

保存树的号码。

记住，柠檬会说话。

蜜蜂——来自菲律宾，在阿拉斯加州诺姆死于 2217 年 4 月 26 日，享年 2.68 亿岁。脱落的冰山碾压了曾在会议室里到处飞的蜜蜂。有一次在一家公司公开募股期间，我和首席执行官、首席财务官和首席运营官差点在一架小型飞机上丧命。落地后，首席执行官瞪了我一眼，好像是我引起了风暴。好像黄色的灯光是我想出来的。好像嗡嗡声是来自我的摇晃。好像闪电是把我绊倒的一个盒子。也许他是对的。也许我已经疏远了自己内心想要活下去的那一部分。那想让大家活下去的部分。就像我永远都和母亲疏远了，除了她的死。

张明鎧——死于 2015 年 8 月 3 日，就是别人父母过世时从不流泪的那个。现在我会提出问题，会随身带着眼镜。我在梦里摇动树木，以便明天和他人一起颤抖。六个兄弟姐妹中，只有一人来参加葬礼，那就是大舅。有几个打来电话、哭了、问了些问题。这个大舅说他知道出了什么事，因为母亲死的那天早上，他感到有人踢他，并认定是她。现在我知道别人也觉得母亲很难相处。但她不是他的母亲。她是我的，就我一个人的。所以对她的愤怒也是我的。我一个人的。对死者的愤怒是桌上已完全膨胀起来的蛋糕。是裹着玻璃的刀。

衣物 —— 死于 2015 年 8 月 10 日。我们把它们塞进花园垃圾袋里，准备捐赠。T 恤衫一件接一件，扣领衫一件接一件，连衣裙接着连衣裙，肢体连着肢体。有些跃入眼帘就像噩梦中的火焰，火焰的形态几乎跟人一样。我把这些留了下来。我把数百支铅笔留了下来。我写字用的就是母亲抽屉里的一支。铅笔上刻着"底特律公立学校"，她曾在那里教过书。写下的每一句话都与我作对。有次我们用轮椅把她推到楼下，玩了槌球和迷你高尔夫。她坐在一旁看着，空洞的眼神看不到我们看到的任何事物。就好像她的目光穿越了我们，穿越了太阳。八月的天已经注定了她能看见而我们看不见。我把她留在太阳底下太久了。一个孩子在草坪上翻筋斗，母亲继续看着，她穿着一件白色的上衣，上面有粉红色小花旋转的图案。我一直盯着她看。我把花留了下来。我把空白的衬衫捐了。

内疚 —— 从未在 2017 年 8 月 3 日死去。我雇了职业杀手去使用导弹。但内疚还在夜里像一堆冰冻的鸽子堆在我胸口。上个月，父亲又摔了一跤。我第三次穿过了他。听说他想跑但被绊倒了。又一次脑出血。我们把他搬到楼上的记忆护理中心，就好像陌生人也会关心他的记忆。我去看他的时候，没人能找到他。我们打开一扇又一扇的门，每个人身上的味道都呈方块状冲了出来。我们发现他躺在别人的床上，头发嗡嗡作响。他把眼镜递给我说："这是我的未来。"我满脑子都在想："我死去的母亲会怎么做？"我挨个房间去找她。能找到的都是肢解的影子和 C 形的躯干，头被掏空了。我能听到黑暗中所有心脏的跳动声。问题是，它们听起来都一样。我自己的心跳也慢了下来。内疚也变成了一颗心脏，混在其间，与其他所有的心脏一起繁殖。

海洋 —— 死于 2017 年 8 月 21 日，当时我没有跳海，而是把门拽上，拉上保险栓。我身体里的水想涌入大海，我想象自己被海水冲刷，分离成点点水滴，我本来的模样。我好几天都能感受到脖子上的盐。我曾经认识的一名女子从窗口跳下，摔死了。区别是，有人追赶她。有科学家说海洋正在变暖。有的说海洋里有缺氧区域。连水都有等级之分。一个孩子的死比一名女子的死更为可怕，除非这名女子是孩子的单亲母亲。如果死去的女子是一位成年人的母亲，那么这不过是"生命的一部分"。如果母女一起死，那是一种"耻辱"。如果一家人都死了，那是一场"灾难"。我们将怎样看待整个海洋的死亡呢？"安息"吧。

脸——与躯干、灰尘和小白骨一起死于2015年8月3日。脸代表人格，是我们最常展示给他人的部分。我能通过母亲的手认出她吗？或是她的脚？在去肯尼迪机场的路上，有一座很古老的墓园，里面的墓碑大小不一，都倾斜着。墓碑代表一个人的脸，与照片代表一张脸不同。鸣笛有某种含义。它让我们抬头向外看火车。火车开的时候，铁轨代表着一种缺失，但也暗示着火车曾经存在过，暗示着希望与回归。也许没有开始。也许没有什么挽歌，就像室内的雨既不是开始也不是结束。

我的孩子们说不，
我说可以，因为我知道。
我告诉她们，她们可以。
但今天，有人被枪杀。
我们走进搅拌机。

*

你有没有
细细地观察过孩子的脸庞，
仔细得能让你看到上帝，
看到一小撮头发，你知道
都会因每一次新的枪击而竖起来？

四　　　　文明的华盖被烧毁。

天空灰暗

如同抛光的鲸骨。但天空中

有火种

无论是来自灯光还是黎明。

有某种骚动——

某处梧桐上的麻雀

在鸣叫。

——弗吉尼亚·伍尔夫《海浪》

美国——死于 2018 年 2 月 14 日，而我死去的母亲却不知道。自从她死后，美国已经经历了一连串的小型死亡，每一次都比上一次更具体。现在，我的眼泪是钩子的形状，而我的心仍然潮湿。幸运的话，还在跳动。不幸死去的孩子们拿着电报，必须交给办公桌前的女士。那位女士会收好他们的遗物和影子。我死去的母亲问每一个孩子是否认识我、见到过我，问我的孩子们现在有多高了。他们会告诉她，他们以前住在佛罗里达州，不在加州。她会去见那个头上有个窟窿的孩子。她会把梦像灰尘一样从窟窿里吹出来。我曾以为死亡是一种麻醉。现在我想象它是长长的队伍，我母亲带着所有的孩子。我想象她抚摸他们的头发。想象她会挠他们的膝盖逗他们笑。死去的人拿着我们手里的另外半张票。死者是风的形象。他们梳头发的时候，我们的树会沙沙作响。

我愿意
承认我爱我的孩子们。
承认这一点
就是承认他们会死。
"死"：除了文字，谁都不懂。

*

孩子们啊，我的孩子们，
这首诗不会结束，因为
我试图
用希望啊希望啊希望来结束这首诗，
看嘴巴是怎样永远张开的？

OBIT

VICTORIA CHANG

POEMS

For my mother and my children.

I

Give sorrow words; the grief that does not speak

wispers the o'er-fraught heart, and bids it break.

—William Shakespeare, *Macbeth*

My Father's Frontal Lobe—died unpeacefully of a stroke on June 24, 2009 at Scripps Memorial Hospital in San Diego, California. Born January 20, 1940, the frontal lobe enjoyed a good life. The frontal lobe loved being the boss. It tried to talk again but someone put a bag over it. When the frontal lobe died, it sucked in its lips like a window pulled shut. At the funeral for his words, my father wouldn't stop talking and his love passed through me, fell onto the ground that wasn't there. I could hear someone stomping their feet. The body is as confusing as language—was the frontal lobe having a tantrum or dancing? When I took my father's phone away, his words died in the plastic coffin. At the funeral for his words, we argued about my miscarriage. *It's not really a baby,* he said. I ran out of words, stomped out to shake the dead baby awake. I thought of the tech who put the wand down, quietly left the room when she couldn't find the heartbeat. I understood then that darkness is falling without an end. That darkness is not the absorption of color but the absorption of language.

My Mother—died unpeacefully on August 3, 2015 in her room at Walnut Village Assisted Living in Anaheim, California of pulmonary fibrosis. The room was born on July 3, 2012. The Village wasn't really a village. No walnut trees. Just cut flowers. Days before, the hospice nurse silently slid the stethoscope on top of my mother's lung and waited for it to inflate. The way waiting becomes an injury. The way the nurse breathed in, closed his eyes, breathed out, and said, *I'm sorry.* Did the blood rush to my face or to my fingertips? Did he reopen his eyes before or after he said, *I'm sorry?* The way memory is the ringing after a gunshot. The way we try to remember the gunshot but can't. The way memory gets up after someone has died and starts walking.

Victoria Chang—died unknowingly on June 24, 2009 on the I-405 freeway. Born in the Motor City, it is fitting she died on a freeway. When her mother called about her father's heart attack, she was living an indented life, a swallow that didn't dip. This was not her first death. All her deaths had creases except this one. It didn't matter that her mother was wrong (it was a stroke) but that Victoria Chang had to ask whether she should drive to see the frontal lobe. When her mother said *yes,* Victoria Chang had the feeling of not wanting to. Someone heard that feeling. Because he did not die but all of his words did. At the hospital, Victoria Chang cried when her father no longer made sense. This was before she understood the cruelty of his disease. It would be the last time she cried in front of it. She switched places with her shadow because suffering changes shape and happens secretly.

Victoria Chang—died unwillingly on April 21, 2017 on a cool day in Seal Beach, California, on her way back from the facility named Sunrise, which she often mistakenly called *Sunset*. Her father's problems now her problems, nailed to her frontal lobe. Like a typist, she tried to translate his problems, carry the words back in a pony carriage one by one. When the pony moved, the letters strung together to form sentences. But when the pony refused to move, the carriage disappeared. The letters tagged her and ran into the cornfields. The police came and shined their lights onto the field, started shooting the letters even though they had their hands up. Sometimes, they shot the letters twice, just to make sure. Sometimes, they shot them in the back. When we shoot a letter once, it's called *typing*. Twice, *engraving*. When someone dies, letters are always engraved. When someone dies, there is a constant feeling of wanting to speak to someone, but the plane with all the words is crossing the sky.

Voice Mail—died on June 24, 2009, the voice mail from my father said *Transcription Beta (low confidence), Hello hi um I may be able to find somebody to reduce the size of the car OK I love you.* The Transcription Beta had low self-esteem. It wandered into the river squinting and came back blind. The Transcription Beta could not transcribe dementia. My father really said, *I'll fold the juice,* not *I love you.* Is language the broom or what's being swept? When I first read *I love you,* some hand spun a fine thread around my lungs and tightened. Because my father had never said that to me before. In the seconds before realization of the error, I didn't feel love, but panic. We read to inherit the words, but something is always between us and the words. Until death, when comprehension and disappearance happen simultaneously.

Language—died, brilliant and beautiful on August 1, 2009 at 2:46 p.m. Lover of raising his hand, language lived a full life of questioning. His favorite was twisting what others said. His favorite was to write the world in black and white and then watch people try and read the words in color. Letters used to skim my father's brain before they let go. Now his words are blind. Are pleated. Are the dispatcher, the dispatches, and the receiver. When my mother was dying, I made everyone stand around the bed for what would be the last group photo. Some of us even smiled. Because dying lasts forever until it stops. Someone said, *Take a few.* Someone said, *Say cheese.* Someone said, *Thank you.* Language fails us. In the way that *breaking an arm* means an arm's bone can break but the arm itself can't break off unless sawed or cut. My mother couldn't speak but her eyes were the only ones that were wide open.

Tankas

My children, children,
there's applesauce everywhere
but it's not for you.
It is strange to help someone
grow while helping someone die.

*

Each time I write *hope,*
the letters fray and scatter.
The hopeful poets
never seem to have my dreams,
never seem to have children.

Language—died again on August 3, 2015 at 7:09 a.m. I heard about my mother's difficult nights. I hired a night person. By the time I got there, she was always gone. The night person had a name but was like a ghost who left letters on my lips. *Couldn't breathe, 2:33 a.m. Screaming, 3:30 a.m. Calm, 4:24 a.m.* I got on all fours, tried to pick up the letters like a child at an egg hunt without a basket. But for every letter I picked up, another fell down, as if protesting the oversimplification of my mother's dying. I wanted the night person to write in a language I could understand. *Breathing unfolding, 2:33. Breathing in blades, 3:30. Breathing like an evening gown, 4:24.* But maybe I am wrong, how death is simply death, each slightly different from the next but the final strike all the same. How the skin responds to a wedding dress in the same way it responds to rain.

Victoria Chang—died on June 24, 2011, at the age of 41. Her imagination lived beyond that day though. It weighed two pounds and could be lifted like weights. Once she brought her father to the arcade. He found the basketball machine and shot one after another. As if he were visiting his past self in prison, touching the clear glass at his own likeness. On the other side of the glass, words like *embankment, unsightly,* and *heterogeneous* lived. He tried to ask his former self for help but the guards wouldn't allow him to pass notes. When the ball machine buzzed, he stopped, eyes deformed and wild. He called my dead mother over to see his score, hand waving at me. What happens when the shadow is attached to the wrong object but refuses to let go? I walked over because I wanted to believe him.

The Future—died on June 24, 2009. A pioneering figure in the past, the future was the president of the present. You are sitting. But the future wants your chair. She is demanding. She is not interested in the spine but what it holds up. She is interested in award ceremonies. She is interested in fallen petals that look like medals. She is interested in anything with the word *track* in it, tenure track, deer tracks, tracksuit, but she doesn't want you to get sidetracked or to backtrack. The future can be thrown away by the privileged. But sometimes she just suddenly dies. The way the second person dies when a mother dies, reborn as third person as *my mother.* The way grief is really about future absence. The way the future closes its offices when a mother dies. What's left: a hole in the ground the size of violence.

Civility—died on June 24, 2009, at the age of 68. Murdered by a stroke whose paintings were recently featured in a museum, two square canvases painted white, black scissors in the middle of each, open, pointing at each other. After my father's stroke, my mother no longer spoke in full sentences. Fragments of codfish, the language of savages, each syllable a mechanical dart from her mouth to my father's holes. Maybe this is what happens when language fails, a last breath inward but no breath outward. A state of holding one's breath forever but not dying. When her lungs began their failing, she could still say *you* but not *thank. You don't know what it's like,* she said when I told her to stop yelling at my father. She was right. When language leaves, all you have left is tone, all you have left are smoke signals. I didn't know she was using her own body as wood.

My Mother's Lungs—began their dying sometime in the past. Doctors talked around tombstones. About the hedges near the tombstones, the font. The obituary writer said the obituary is the moment when someone becomes history. What if my mother never told me stories about the war or about her childhood? Does that mean none of it happened? No one sits next to my mother's small rectangular tombstone, flush to the earth. The stone is meant to be read from above. What if I'm in space and can't read it? Does that mean she didn't die? She died at 7:07 a.m. PST. It is three hours earlier in Hawaii. Does that mean in Hawaii she hasn't died yet? But the plane ride to Hawaii is five hours long. This time gap can never be overcome. The difference is called grieving.

Privacy—died on December 4, 2015. My child brought a balloon that said *Get Well Soon* to the gravesite. This time Peter Manning lay next to my mother. A stranger so close to her. Before this other stone appeared, my mother's stone was still my mother because of the absence around her. The appearance of the new stone and the likeness to her stone implied my mother was a stone too, that my mother was buried under the stone too. On the day of the burial, I hired a Chinese priest. I couldn't understand many of his words because they were not about food. The men who had dug up the dirt stood with their shovels and waited. I looked at their eyes for any sign of drowning. Then I noticed that one man's body didn't have a shadow. And when he walked away, the grass didn't flatten. His shovel was clean. I suddenly recognized this man as love.

My Mother's Teeth—died twice, once in 1965, all pulled out from gum disease. Once again on August 3,2015. The fake teeth sit in a box in the garage. When she died, I touched them, smelled them, thought I heard a whimper. I shoved the teeth into my mouth. But having two sets of teeth only made me hungrier. When my mother died, I saw myself in the mirror, her words around my mouth, like powder from a donut. Her last words were in English. She asked for a Sprite. I wonder whether her last thought was in Chinese. I wonder what her last thought was. I used to think that a dead person's words die with them. Now I know that they scatter, looking for meaning to attach to like a scent. My mother used to collect orange blossoms in a small shallow bowl. I pass the tree each spring. I always knew that grief was something I could smell. But I didn't know that it's not actually a noun but a verb. That it moves.

I tell my children
that hope is like a blue skirt,
it can twirl and twirl,
that men like to open it,
take it apart, and wound it.

*

I tell my children
that sometimes I too can hope,
that sometimes nothing
moves but my love for someone,
and the light from the dead star.

Friendships—died June 24, 2009, once beloved but not consistently beloved. The mirror won the battle. I am now imprisoned in the mirror. All my selves spread out like a deck of cards. It's true, the grieving speak a different language. I am separated from my friends by gauze. I will drive myself to my own house for the party. I will make small talk with myself, spill a drink on myself. When it's over, I will drive myself back to my own house. My conversations with other parents about children pass me on the way up the staircase and repeat on the way down. Before my mother's death, I sat anywhere. Now I look for the image of the empty chair near the image of the empty table. An image is a kind of distance. An image of me sits down. Depression is a glove over the heart. Depression is an image of a glove over the image of a heart.

Gait—my father's gait died on March 14, 2011. Once erect, light, flat- footed. Magnificent. Now, his gait shuffles like sandpaper. Once my father erected a basketball net, mounted it onto a wooden pole from the lumberyard to save money. With each shot, the pole moved a little, invisible to the eye, until I had to shoot from the side of the driveway. Now I avoid semicolons. I look for statues whose eyes don't move with me. The kind of people who stand in place and lights can be strung on. The problem is, my father's brain won't stop walking, and my dead mother is everywhere.

Logic—my father's logic died on June 24, 2009 in bright daylight. Murdered in the afternoon. I hung up Missing Person posters of myself and listened for the sound of a tree falling. The sound of the wind through trees is called *psithurism.* There's no word for the translator of wind. If the wind is words, the trees are exclamation points. The spears of moonlight, question marks. My father doesn't realize his words always end in prepositions. *I have a problem with [the moon], there is a problem between [the moon and me], the problem is on [the moon].* What if he can no longer find what is being modified, in the way snow would fall forever if there were no lip to die on.

Optimism—died on August 3, 2015, a slow death into a pavement. At what point does a raindrop accept its falling? The moment the cloud begins to buckle under it or the moment the ground pierces it and breaks its shape? In December, my mother had her helper prepare a Chinese hot-pot feast. My mother said it would probably be her last Christmas. I laughed at her. She yelled at my father all night. I put a fish ball in my mouth. My optimism covered the whole ball as if the fish had never died, had never been gutted and rolled into a humiliating shape. To acknowledge death is to acknowledge that we must take another shape.

Ambition—died on August 3, 2015, a sudden death. I buried ambition in the forest, next to distress. They used to take walks together until ambition pushed distress off the embankment. Now, they put a bracelet around my father's ankle. The alarm rings when he gets too close to the door. His ambitious nature makes him walk to the door a lot. When the alarm rings, he gets distressed. He remembers that he wants to find my house. He thinks he can find my house. His fingerprints have long vanished from my house. Some criminals put their fingers on electric coils of a stove to erase their fingerprints. But it only makes them easier to find. They found my father in the middle of the road last month, still like a bulbless lamp, unable to recall its function, confused like the moon. At the zoo, a great bald eagle sits in a small cage because of a missing wing. Its remaining wing is grief. Above the eagle, a bird flying is the eagle's memory, and its prey, the future.

Chair—my mother's green chair died on August 3, 2015. We arrange chairs in rows facing the same direction to represent reverence. In a circle to represent sharing. Stacked to represent completion. Hanging from the ceiling to represent art. In front of a desk to represent work. Before my mother died, I routed all her mail to my house. Her catalogues still come every day. I imagine her sitting in her chair flipping through them for more shirts that look the same. I understand now, only the living change clothes. Last week, I took my father pants-shopping. I heard him quarreling with the pants. He came out of the dressing room with his pants on backwards. Two pockets facing forward, like my mother's eyes mocking me, as if to say, *I told you so.* He was angry, pointing and cursing at the *chairs* that no longer fit. I entered the men's dressing room and picked up all the pants on the floor because one of them had to be my missing father.

Do you smell my cries?
They come from another place.
The cry comes from you.
Now everything comes from you.
To be empty and so full.

*

I tell my children
that they can wake anything,
that they are not yet
dying. But what do I know?
I know that a mother dies.

Tears—died on August 3, 2016. Once we stopped at a Vons to pick up flowers and pinwheels on our way to the graveyard. It had been a year and death no longer glittered. My ten-year-old putting the flowers perfectly in the small narrow hole in front of the stone. How she somehow knew what the hole was for, that my mother wasn't really on the other side. Suddenly, our sobbing. How many times have I looked into the sky for some kind of message, only to find content but no form. She ran back to the car. The way grief takes many forms, as tears or pinwheels. The way the word *haystack* never conjures up the same image twice. The way we assume all tears taste the same. The way our sadness is plural, but grief is singular.

Memory—died August 3, 2015. The death was not sudden but slowly over a decade. I wonder if, when people die, they hear a bell. Or if they taste something sweet, or if they feel a knife cutting them in half, dragging through the flesh like sheet cake. The caretaker who witnessed my mother's death quit. She holds the memory and images and now they are gone. For the rest of her life, the memories are hers. She said my mother couldn't breathe, then took her last breath twenty seconds later. The way I have imagined a kiss with many men I have never kissed. My memory of my mother's death can't be a memory but is an imagination, each time the wind blows, leaves unfurl a little differently.

Language—died on March 4, 2017. It wanted to live as long as possible in its form, an icicle on the edge of a roof. I lifted the roof off my father's head and found the balcony to stand on. I spoke loudly and slowly about the Guggenheim. Two women at the table across from us with plates of all-you-can-eat snow crab legs, their fourth each. I repeated myself again and again. The women kept getting up for more, their sucking noises like eating an overripe peach. My father finally said that he would like to *see a copy of the pamphlet.* This year they sent a spacecraft on a suicide mission between Saturn and its rings. If I could get between my father and his brain, would I too be committing suicide? If someone is directing the spacecraft, isn't it murder? The pictures sent back are silent. A picture represents a moment that has died. Then every photo is a crime scene. When we remember the dead, at some point, we are remembering the picture, not the moment.

Tomas Tranströmer—died on March 26, 2015, at the age of 83. He wrote: *I am carried in my shadow / like a violin / in its black case. // The only thing I want to say / glitters out of reach / like the silver / in a pawnbroker's.* My father couldn't have written those words before or after his stroke. I wonder if his daughters disliked visiting him as much as I dislike visiting my father. The way his fists stay shut, the way his mind is always out of earshot. The way his words abandon his mouth and each day I pick them up, put them back in, screw the lid on tighter. Sometimes when he complains and no one can understand, I think of all the places I hid as a child. All the times I have silenced someone by covering their mouth with mine.

Approval—died on August 3, 2015 at the age of 44. It died at 7:07 a.m. *How much money will you get* was my mother's response to everything. She used to wrap muffins in a napkin at the buffet and put them in her purse. I never saw the muffins again. What I would do to see those muffins again, the thin moist thread as she pulled the muffin apart. A photo shows my mother holding my hand. I was nine. I never touched her hand again. Until the day before she died. I love so many things I have never touched: the moon, a shiver, my mother's heart. Her fingers felt like rough branches covered with plastic. I trimmed her nails one by one while the morphine kept her asleep. Her nails weren't small moons or golden doors to somewhere, but ten last words I was cutting off.

Sometimes all I have
are words and to write them means
they are no longer
prayers but are now animals.
Other people can hunt them.

*

You don't need a thing
from me, you already have
everything you need:
the moon, a wound on the lake,
our footprints to not follow.

Secrets—died on August 7, 2015 and they were relieved to die. No one at the funeral had known about my mother's illness. No one had known how fiercely my mother and father fought. One Chinese face after another. I told the story. Told it again. Their mouths opened like time. Red sashes with Chinese characters I couldn't read. The stems spoke with their flowers. To look down and see their legs missing. Later, I found a photo of my mother smiling with friends at her home, just the year before. No oxygen tank, no tube in her nose. She must have taken it off, put it in the closet between the beginning of her life and the end of her life. I imagine her panicking inside, waiting for them to leave. The mind and speech assemble and disassemble like geese. Scientists now say that a mind still works after the body has died. That there's a burst of brain energy. Then maybe she heard the geese above disassemble one last time. Then maybe my kiss on her cheek felt like lightning.

Music—died on August 7, 2015. I made a video with old pictures and music for the funeral. I picked "Hallelujah" in a cappella. Because they weren't really singing, but actually crying. When my children came into the room, I pretended I was writing. Instead, I looked at my mother's old photos. The fabric patterns on all her shirts. The way she held her hands together at the front of her body. In each picture, the small brown purse that now sits under my desk. At the funeral, my brother-in-law kept turning the music down. When he wasn't looking, I turned the music up. Because I wanted these people to feel what I felt. When I wasn't looking, he turned it down again. At the end of the day, someone took the monitor and speakers away. But the music was still there. This was my first understanding of grief.

Appetite—died its final death on Father's Day, June 21, 2015, peacefully and quietly among family. We dressed my mother, rolled her down in her wheelchair. The oxygen machine breathing like an animal. They were the only Chinese people at the facility. The center table was loud again, was invite-only again. Like always, I filled my mother's plates with food. Her favorite colored puddings contained in plastic cups. When we got up to leave, her food still there, glistening like worms. No one thought much of it. There are moments that are like brushstrokes, when only much later after the ocean is finished, become the cliff's edge that they were all along. Death is our common ancestor. It doesn't care whom we have dined with.

Appetite—died on March 16, 2015. Once, in graduate school, I was the only one to order a drink at the restaurant. My boyfriend did not like this. He dropped me off in the middle of town to walk home. I looked at the children's clothing in the window, the little striped cap, pink dress, and thought about beauty. I spun around to avoid darkness but darkness was the one spinning me. I hid in a bright Taco Bell. The man at the register had a narrow hole for a mouth and a brown mass on his cheek. He was so beautiful that I thought he must be Death. Twenty years later, my mother requested Taco Bell for lunch. I ran out to buy her bags and bags of tacos. No one in line understood my emergency. The man I handed my credit card to had a brown mass on his face. He nodded when he handed me the bag, as if he knew. My mother pressed her lips to the tacos, as if she were kissing someone for the rapturous last time.

Form—died on August 3, 2015. My children sleep with framed photos of my mother. Leaden, angular, metal frames. My ten-year-old puts her frame in the red velvet bag that held the cremation urn and brings it with her on vacation. A photo of my mother sits in the bag that once held a container of her ashes. When we die, we are represented by representations of representations, often in different forms. Memories too are representations of the dead. I go through corridors looking for the original but can't find her. In Palm Springs, the desert fails me. Dust, sand, gravel, bits of dead things everywhere, a speck of someone else's dead mother blows into my eye and I start crying again. The heat is now too optimistic. The pool and its luster like an inquisition. My own breathing, between the splashes and children laughing, no longer a miracle, but simple mathematics.

Optimism—died on August 3, 2015, of monotony. Before my sister would fly home, she and my mother would cry together. The one time my mother cried to me, I said, *The doctor's wrong, you don't know how long—it could be a year or more.* She didn't stop crying. I got up and left the room. Outside, three floors below, behind the building, a family was celebrating something in their yard. Piñatas, music, children momentarily suspended above Earth in a bounce house. That summer, we were not on Earth, but pacing in a building above it. People in a city can spend a lifetime never actually touching the earth once. I was so afraid their happiness would rise up through the window like steam. I could hear the thumping of the sticks on the piñata, once a happy anticipation, altered to the inevitability of the candy dropping. Now I close my eyes and try to remember the optimism of the thumping, the origin of things.

I can't say with faith
that I would run toward a bus
to save you from death.
If a girl is only as
good as her mother, then what?

*

To love anyone
means to admit extinction.
I tell myself this
so I never fall in love,
so that the fire lights just me.

Hands—died on January 13, 2015. My mother's handwriting had become jagged and shaky. Bodies jump out of bed. Feet leap off of bridges. Hands never leap. They flag people down. They gesture to enhance language. They are the last part of hugging, which the body mostly does. They wipe off the tears that the eyes release. They write on paper the things the brain sends. After my mother died, I looked at a photo where she had moved into assisted living from the ER. Her oxygen tube in her nose, my two small children standing on each side. Her hands around their hands pulled tightly to her chest, the chorus of knuckles still housed, white stones, soon to be freed, soon to be splashing.

Oxygen—died on March 12, 2012. At first, it came in heavy green canisters. Then a large rolling machine that pushed air day and night. When my mother changed her clothes, she had to take the tube out of her nose. She stopped to catch her breath, as if breath were constantly in motion, as if it could be chased. I'm not sure when I began to notice her panic without the oxygen, in the way we don't notice a leaf turning red or an empire falling. One day, it just appears, as if it had been there all along. Like the hospice staff with their papers, bags of medicine, their garlands of silence. Like grief, the way it dangles from everything like earrings. The way grief needs oxygen. The way every once in a while, it catches the light and starts smoking. The way my grief will die with me. The way it will cleave and grow like antlers.

Reason—died on June 24, 2009, like make-believe trees, that just get taken down and put away. My father's words taken out of his brain and left downstairs. Remote but close, like a wound on your child or a curtain blowing in the other room. This week, he is obsessed with the scheduled walks again. This week he doesn't want to wait for the other much older but sharper residents. The memory of reason is there, of once pulling the ropes. When reason dies, determination does not. As in, my father is determined to walk at 10 a.m. at a certain pace. As in his body is determined to move forward with or without his brain, which is two empty slippers nailed into the ground.

Home—died on January 12, 2013. The first of five moves meant the boxes were still optimistic that they would be opened. They were still stiff, arrogant about their new shape, flatness just a memory. At the new house, my father on one of his obsessive walks found the one old Chinese person, a bony lady with branches for teeth, the kind of woman my mother would normally shun because of her background. She visited my mother every day for a year. She brought oranges, vegetables, a salesperson from a funeral home. My father left them to speak in Chinese as he wandered the neighborhood so he wouldn't die. The lady swore at my father in Chinese. Called him *stupid*. A *fool*. At the funeral, she said, *God brought me here to help your mother.* And it struck me. My father's words were an umbrella that couldn't open. My mother held the umbrella, refused to let the wind take it. And this old woman was the wind.

Memory—died on July 11, 2015. When I returned from a trip, my mother on the edge of the bed, hair mostly white, black dye underneath, like a memory. Sheets off the bed in a corner like crushed birds. The caretaker hadn't come for a week. My father pacing, his hands tried to speak for him. Too much pressure on the hands. No one knew what happened that week but the hands. My mother had soiled herself. It was all over her hair that she had rolled in pink curlers one by one her whole life. She denied the soiling. Yelled at me in Chinese for saying it. My child and I bathed her as she sat on the shower chair, naked, slumped over, a defeated animal. Death was still abstract, it could slip down the drain. Sadness was still indivisible. In twenty-three days, it would detonate and shower us like confetti. The water flattened my mother's hair and began burying her tongue.

II

Let the stars
Plummet to their dark address,

Let the mercuric
Atoms that cripple drip
Into the terrible well,

You are the one
Solid the spaces lean on, envious.
You are the baby in the barn.

—Sylvia Plath, from "Nick and the Candlestick"

I Am a Miner. The Light Turns Blue.

A herd of   ribs   ripped   the   eggs
out   of   us   what's left   thousands
of wingless bees   that shake in place that no
longer make   goods   that no longer   think
clearly   drunk stripes   collide figures on the TV
rub like   driftwood   babies' heads   turn
toward them   shapes that have   separated   from
their   bodies   everything is drifting   the frames
of the houses   are missing   what's left drapes like a
shirt mothers sit underneath and   sew water   here
the pages are   turning but no one is   reading   here
we are   not talented   here we are   torrential and
babies are always growing   here one light   in one
house on   one street beats on   in   pain
*

If they say that   happiness is   water   that it
is always   growing   then my kind   must be the
lunar crater kind   circular in its shape stingy in its   flow
sometimes I cannot   control its   shedding its   rebellion
other times it flash freezes and I chip away   with an
ice pick until my   fingers   freeze into an   artichoke

a man with a stroller says   it's worth it   but   it feels

like   hooves on my face   I   cannot   bench-press it

I want a   fixed income of you   so   I can tell you   I don't

want   you to stay   I want   to wake   each

morning   and   find   your   cloth figure next   to me

I want   to prick you and   paw   you   I want to

be   your inseam   to   tailor you   to   wear

you to   be   you

*

If you are   the portobello   we are the   undersides

of   portobellos   the keyed-in lips   even

desire is   split   stained glass   divides

our faces   into   abundance   each day   we

are   redivided   each day   we try to   push our

selves   back together   like grass   each day   the night

detonates   tries to stick   itself to   morning   light

each day   we are   renamed like a new   monsoon

we are sculled again   and   again as   saline is

hit by drips   each   strike   different   from

the next   here   we are   sick but   have no

symptoms   here the   rain   is always crowded

here we   always   wear   gowns   with

open backs but   don't know   why

*

An old man   pushes up   a clavicle of a lime tree

only the   ashes know why   they   fall from his

cigarette like   asterisks he doesn't look up   our bodies

and   strollers overlap   fresh cement steams   against

stucco homes and new sod   babies' faces   reflect on

storefronts   our skin   like   cactuses   we are

latched to   this   landscape   where trees   need

wooden sticks to   stand   straight where workers trim

thistles   on the trail   each day working   their way

west   and   back   where fields are   aerated into

Chinese checker boards   plugs of   brown dirt strewn

like   confetti like something to   celebrate   where

we try to shed   ruin   at daylight   but   by   nightfall

our   hands are always wilderness

*

I am a clubfoot   twisted in   inverted   down I am

the one in every   one thousand   sandstorm a man

said you should be   happy look at the   child you

have   but if happiness   is   within the   child

then happiness   runs   away   up the   ladder

through the blue tunnel   down the   slide

164

I want   straightness   unbending   I chase my

other foot like   a lottery   I search to be the one-in-

ten-million winner   power to my powerball my mega

of millions   my factorial   capability   factoring in

the wind   the windows and the probability of   rain

what's left in my winnings   is always this   I want to go

home now   I want my own   room forever   I want

what I used to have   I want   what I have

*

In the last parking lot   in the last city   there are

trees that   look   like nerve endings   scalps of   leaves

thousands of birds in   threes   somewhere   the

last people   have   stopped to   place   white rocks over

dried volcano Beth loves   Jim and   someone loves

Matt   at the last party   the   light   lanced onto

the last baby's   face its body still   slumping   in

ignorance   once while teaching a   child how   to draw

a person   I learned we are made   only of circles and

rectangles I now know   a body must   loosen before

it tightens   I now know a body   can loosen   and

tighten with   many men I now know   Earth   is a

hole   not a   sphere   meant to be   filled

with bodies   not with   thinking

*

Circular saws   grinding gristle   tightening time

I wonder whether   time is running away from

death   or toward death   I   wonder   whether

death   sounds this way or whether death   has

no sound   the food truck   blows   its horn the

sun pushes   and   pushes   nine   mothers with

strollers   babies sit upright like kites   the statue of

a woman has   a space   where the   heart should be

through the space   on the other side of   the park is

an American flag   a man must have made this statue

we are always looking   through   women the men

are nearly done building   the wall   stone   by

stone   we have   wiped drops of milk   off of

lips and   entertained   the   treetops

*

Yesterday I had my   own room with   my own

milkweed but I didn't   want   to be   there

downstairs a baby rolled   across the floor for

the first time like dawn she laughed   clapped

then cried as she   rolled into   the couch in gaining

control she   loses control   I dreamed   that I

166

could finally   leave the house   but I had to

travel through   an alley of bees   the alley was

six feet wide   the bees were six inches long   they

buzzed in   my spine   led me north led me to a town

where everyone worked near apple trees where no one

made flags   where   everyone learned how to multiply

silence how to divide   sadness into small   parcels

how to   gather   colors and give them   away

*

Everyone wanted poems with an emperor a head

looped inside a rope   but this   poem is   tepid   this

poem is no epic   the trail the   hedge   a man on a

tractor digging   divots out of a   field   as if   the

field is   just a field   and not   flesh   one   by

one   the bugs like small   beans lift   out of   the

grass   there is   no other way   thousands

of them   they recede   into balls when   kicked

worm bodies that   roll like earth   they are voiceless

but we cannot   extinguish their screams a grotesque

story but not a   big story   there is   war even here

there is a metal machine there is   a senseless task

there is terror   our   disregard and billions of

bodies rushing   out   like smoked   bees

*

We are disregarding   planets again   Pluto is no
longer one they say   in a show of hands   where
are the bodies if   all the hands   go on deck   when
the hands return how   do they find   their bodies
all around the earth   people spend   one year
chanting   hands hands   fingers thumbs dum ditty
dum ditty   dum dum dum   unlike sharks   we
do not hunt   by   hearing each other's   hearts
we hunt   with our   hands   how our   hands are
always   behind   a wheel on a road that divides
pines   into   tribes   on Saturday   someone's
hand will   tighten the   noose   around another
man's neck   we   will write about it with   our hands
that can't however they   try remain housed   like a heart
*

The rain is   undressed   from the sky   the soil
opens   takes   rain in   as if   it has   the
answers   because the soil   has no   choice
because   the soil is   assaulted too   there   are
diamonds   deep in   the   forest of   soil
pustules   of   God   if you heat a   diamond at

168

high temperatures it   will   dissolve   into thin

air like   a   woman   there are   diamonds

beneath a   baby's foot and   its soft nail clippings

here   the rain does   not have   a mouth   it is

more slap   than tongue   congrats the cards say

hand wash me   your   little mouth   says

as it   kisses   me   the raindrops   reflect

my face   into   millions   of   yous

*

If darkness   could be   combed there would be

hundreds of   knots   morning and   night

cross on the   concrete   a snail   flattened

into the   shape of a   scream a fish has broken

from the   water   its   rod of a body   flickers on

the dirt   walkers cross   over   its   eye

somewhere a child   tries to   wake   up   by

thrashing its body   somewhere bugs grip   thugs

of dirt   and the worms   look more   beautiful

dead   a bee   catches on a   stroller's wheel and

crackles   as if   its heart can   be   broken   if we

push   the wheel   forward   we   ignore death if

we walk backwards   we repeat   death   so we

stand still   and try to   outlast   death

*

Two life-sized tarp   snowmen   held   still by

strings   bleeding light on a lawn   deer   with

moving heads and   little bulbs   look   at him

climbing   up   and down the ladder   a ladder that

begins   and ends   differently the bottom   can

hear   the worms coming   out   of   the soil

the top sees   the dust on the   underside of a

moon   it is both dust and   a metaphor for

marriage   I hate the lawn   the snowmen   the

carrot nose the   queasy smile   the end of   nature but

I know nothing   the baby sees   the glow the

snowmen and   laughs   how can I explain Easter then

we paint the eggs   we hide the eggs   we find the eggs

we put salt on   them   and we   eat   them

*

A spider works each   day   not to   make beauty

but to eat   how the human mind is   detached

from the heart at   the perfect   distance   the distance

is how   we don't see   everything as   beauty

the difference   between   the spider   and   us is   we

can   let   things live   For Sale signs on lawns   shadows rising but   sinking   once we pass   summer   has

wounded   the empty   beef jerky bag erased

half of   someone's list   near the gutter   what's

left   *brown*   *umber*   *cottage*   the mystery is

how   the list seems   placed with   such

care   as one   might prop   a batch of lilacs

against   the roadside   and how   we   know

the flowers   don't   represent   beauty

*

I am   thinking   about happiness again how

you are in some   alternate orthography   perhaps you

are the   raised bumps in braille   perhaps your presence

allows   me to   examine the low   pressure area

the part that often   brings rain   without the clapping

and the   murmurs that are you   how would I   see an

echo   as   anything   other than grieving   light is here but

it is a complement   what is the sun but   a source of

light and   what is light   but a wavelength   detectable by

the eye   light is not   happiness   I seek the underside

of you   the mossy   dark follicle side   light includes

everything   it is perfectly   bound   and because perfect

darkness is   impossible   to create   I seek it as an eye

seeks the   black   cavity of   another eye

*

Another   morning   finally   a man is   hired to
drag   a metal grid over   a dirt path as if   dirt   too
needs   to be   tamed   another man is   speed
walking   arms   beating   the photo on   his
lanyard faded   his eyes in a truce   a woman so thin
she has no   face   blank from running marathons
her   body remembers   pain in a   different way than
it remembers   suffering   pain is a   sail on a boat
suffering are many distant sails   she passes a baby in
a stroller   reaching for his   toes   he is practicing how
to grab   a   girl   how far can   a girl   run
into   the woods   a girl can   run   halfway
into   the woods   from then on   she is   trying
to run   out   of   the woods

*

If a man is   earth   then a woman is   a beaker
that   sits on   earth   on a stack of   other
beakers in a   cabinet   in a school   if a
woman   is a   beaker   then a   baby is a watch
glass   that covers   her evenly that   doesn't
completely   seal her so gases can still   exchange

172

if a baby is a   watch glass   then   poetry is

the   moon   that tries to   slope   its light

through the   watch glass   into   an   undividable

glare   graduating down the side   like a   tassel

up over   the watch glass   leaving   drops

that   bloom   like   frost on a   shrub

expanding   everything   underneath   in

white   blaze

*

The end of   running   of ambition is   a loaf of

hard white   bread   unbladed on   a wooden table

I still want to cut   the bread   to eat the bread but

it's   too late   I still want to   shake the   saltshaker

pregnant in the shape of a   snowman   the disfigured

the hardened the simple the snowman's eyes are not a

window they are stillborn as   paper   here there are no

Greek gods   just   the spiky cries of a   baby and the

private legend of   her birth   here success is not having

a wax figure made   of you   its mucous spit   skin flakes

kisses turn to   rashes   rashes ruffle around   wrists

in the end of   ambition there is snow shaped   like

faith   dice   to   give   away   the end of everything

masculine   and vials   and vials   of joy

III

For last year's words belong to last year's language.
And next year's words await another voice.

—T.S. Eliot, *Four Quartets*

Friendships—died a slow death after August 3, 2015. The friends visited my father. They sat in chairs and spoke Chinese. Wore dictionaries for coats. Strange looks between spouses. The friends went home feeling good that they had done their duty, picked up odds and ends of words. Each had memories of offices, of seeing the other side of the sun. The visits lessened and lessened. They were being pursued by their own deaths. I wonder about the leaves and their relationship with fruit. Do the leaves care about the swelling of the fruit? Does the fruit consider the leaves while it expands? Maybe the leaves shade the fruit as it grows and the fruit emits fragrance for the leaves. But eventually, each must face its own falling alone.

Caretakers—died in 2009, 2010, 2011, 2012, 2013, 2014, 2015, 2016, 2017, one after another. One didn't show up because her husband was arrested. Most others watched the clock. Time breaks for the living eventually and we can walk out of doors. The handle of time's door is hot for the dying. What use is a door if you can't exit? A door that can't be opened is called a wall. On the other side, glass can bloom. My father is on the other side of the wall. Tomatoes are ripening on the other side. I can see them through the window that also can't be opened. A window that can't be opened is just a see-through wall. Sometimes we're on the inside as on a plane. Most of the time, we're on the outside looking in such as doggie day care. I don't know if the tomatoes are the new form of his language or if they're simply for eating. I can't ask him because on the other side, there are no words. All I can do is stare at the nameless bursting tomatoes and know they have to be enough.

Subject Matter—always dies, what we are left with is architecture, form, sound, all in a room, darkened, a few chairs unarranged. The door is locked from the inside. But still, subject matter breaks in and all the others rise. My mother's death is not her story. My father's stroke is not his story. I am not my mother's story, not my father's story. But there is a meeting place that is hidden, one that holds all the maps toward indifference. Can pain be separated from subject matter? Can subject matter take flight and lose its way, peck on another tree? How do you walk heavily with subject matter on your back, without trampling all the meadows?

Sadness—dies while the man across the street trims the hedges and I can see my children doing cartwheels. Or in the moment I sit quietly and listen to the sky, consider the helicopter or the child's hoarse breathing at night. Time after a death changes shape, it rolls slightly downhill as if it knows to move itself forward without our help. Because after a death, there is no *moving on* despite the people waving us through the broken lights. There is only a stone key that fits into one stone lock. But the dead are holding the key. And the stone is a boulder in a stream. I wave my memories in, beat them with a wooden spoon, just for a moment, to stop the senselessness of time, the merriment, just for a moment to feel the tinsel of death again, its dirty bloody beak.

Empathy—died sometime before January 20, 2017. The gate vanished but we don't know when. The doorbell vanished. The trains stopped moving. Someone stole the North Pole sign. I am you, and you, and you. But there are so many obstacles between us. I can never feel my mother's illness or my father's dementia. The black notes on the score are only representations of sound, the keys must knock certain strings which are made of steel, steel is made of iron and carbon from the earth. Why do we make things like a piano that try to represent beauty or pain? Why must we always draw what we see? *Just copy it,* my mother used to say about drawing. The artist is only visiting pain, imagining it. We praise the artist, not the apple, not the apple's shadow which is murdered slowly. There must be some way of drawing a picture so that it doesn't become an elegy.

The Obituary Writer—can die before the subject. John Wilson died in 2002, before the publication of his obituary on bandleader Artie Shaw who died in 2004. What if I die before my father? I've written his obituary in my head every day since his stroke. My father's brain has died before him. It was surrounded by his beloved skull. What if the hinges on his skull break and the brain falls out? Do I give it back or toss it? What if we call the waiter over and God comes instead? Do we offer Him a seat and a brandy or do we cover our eyes and hope He doesn't see us? My mother spent years knowing she would die. But in her last days, she had no idea. To suffer for so long with knowledge but not to finish what was known. Why do I need her to know in her last moments? Like the people who died in the Oakland warehouse fire, crawling on the floor, trying to sort between a battered organ and a door, between a staircase and a shadow. Death isn't the enemy. Knowledge of death is the enemy.

Do you see the tree?
Its secrets grow as lemons.
Sometimes I pretend
I love my children more than
words—no one knows this but words.

*

My children, children,
today my hands are dreaming
as they touch your hair.
Your hair turns into winter.
When I die, your hair will snow.

The Doctors—died on August 3, 2015, surrounded by all the doctors before them and their eyes that should have been red but weren't. The Russian doctor knew death was near before anyone else, first said the word *hospice,* a word that looks like *hospital* and *spice.* Which is it? To yearn for someone's quick death seems wrong. To go to the hospital cafeteria and hunch over a table of toast, pots of jam, butter glistening seems wrong. To want to extend someone's life who is suffering seems wrong. Do we want the orchid or the swan swimming in the middle of the lake? We can touch the orchid and it doesn't move. The orchid is our understanding of death. But the swan is death.

Yesterday—died at midnight. All gold. Wet handkerchiefs from mourning. John Updike once said, E*ach day, we wake slightly altered, and the person we were yesterday is dead. So why, one could say, be afraid of death, when death comes all the time?* Updike must not have watched someone slowly suffocating. Our air goes in and out like silk in the folders of the lungs. But breathing is a lucky accident. Updike must not have seen Death bring glasses of water but not speak. He must have never carried time over his shoulders as it bled. I think he would change his mind, now having gone through death. His words might no longer come out as birds, but as bandages. The living seem to be the only ones who hypothesize about death. The only ones who try to lift it up.

Grief—as I knew it, died many times. It died trying to reunite with other lesser deaths. Each morning I lay out my children's clothing to cover their grief. The grief remains but is changed by what it is covered with. A picture of oblivion is not the same as oblivion. My grief is not the same as my pain. My mother was a mathematician so I tried to calculate my grief. My father was an engineer so I tried to build a box around my grief, along with a small wooden bed that grief could lie down on. The texts kept interrupting my grief, forcing me to speak about nothing. If you cut out a rectangle of a perfectly blue sky, no clouds, no wind, no birds, frame it with a blue frame, place it face up on the floor of an empty museum with an open atrium to the sky, that is grief.

Doctors—died on July 16, 2014. Dr. Lynch was supposed to be the best. I researched. I called. I asked. I read. All my schooling had prepared me to help my mother. I was the youngest and most educated child of Death. A hundred people in the waiting room all pulling green oxygen cylinders. I had all the air to myself but I couldn't breathe. We waited two hours. The doctor wore a blue banker shirt, silky red tie that covered his lungs. My mother pointed at me, *I want to live longer so I can spend more time with her.* I think she meant my children, what I represented. The doctor clipped the X-rays to the little box of light. His pen pointed to all the extra dark spots. I was supposed to feel something as he spoke. I looked away because I've never looked at the insides of my mother before. The seeing was the wrong way. I know now that to be loved as a child means to be watched. In high school, I loved when the teacher turned the lights off. A moment to feel loved and unseen at once. I understand now. We can't be loved when the lights are off.

Blame—wants to die but cannot. Its hair is untidy but it's always here. My mother blamed my father. I blamed my father's dementia. My father blamed my mother's lack of exercise. My father is the story, not the storyteller. I eventually blamed my father because the story kept on trying to become the storyteller. Blame has no face. I have walked on its staircase around and around, trying to slap its face but only hitting my own cheeks. When some people suffer, they want to tell everyone about their suffering. When the brush hits a knot, the child cries out loud, makes a noise that is an expression of pain but not the pain itself. I can't feel the child's pain but some echo of her pain, based on my imagination. Blame is just an echo of pain, a veil across the face of the one you blame. I blame God. I want to complain to the boss of God about God. What if the boss of God is rain and the only way to speak to rain is to open your mouth to the sky and drown?

Time—died on August 3, 2015. A week before my mother died, the nurse called and said to *be prepared.* I looked through my purse for the rest of the words. My pockets empty. Prepared for what? Could I prepare if the words were missing? Is a stem with a bud considered a flower? A bud is not a flower but a soon-to-be flower. No word exists for *about to die* but *dying* but even dying lacks time in the same way a bud lacks a timeline. My mother thought it was only an infection. She blamed them for not giving her antibiotics sooner. But time was ahead of her, the wheel already turning. The nurse said after, *I'm surprised she made it through the weekend.* I was surprised she died at all. Time isn't a moment. Time is enlarged, blurry. As in, my ten-year-old wrapped my dead mother's bracelet for her own birthday and said it was a gift.

Today I show you
the people living in tents.
If you lean in and
listen, the lemon makes noise,
pound your fist and it will fall.

*

My children, children,
do you know a dead heart chimes?
That my breath is an
image that you will forget,
you will lift it like a sheet.

Form—died on August 3, 2015. After my mother died, the weather got hotter so gradually we all became blind. Another bird fell out of the ficus, left its eggs. The arm that turned the earth never bothered to stop for the bird and the bird was crushed between the earth and time. After my mother died, my love for her lost all shape. Everything I had disliked about her became fibrous. I let them harden and suffocate. I posted about her last days on an online pulmonary fibrosis board, typing to strangers into the night, the edges of our fingertips touching. That story is still there but I can no longer find it or the people who might be dead. Each letter a small soldier in formation for a new dying person to read, to see how the living might perceive them when they are unconscious. Grief isn't what spills out of a cracked egg. Grief is the row of eggs waiting in the cold to lose their shape.

Control—died on August 3, 2015, along with my mother. Suddenly I was no longer in the middle of the earth. Suddenly I could change the angle of the liquid pen so that the rocket went the other way. And all the children stopped crying. My sister set up the appointment with the neurologist who asked, *What's your name?* My father said, *What what the system is... what,* as he reached into his wallet and gave the doctor his credit card. His finger angrily pointing at me. We left with prescriptions for my father— antidepressants, antianxiety, anger-management pills. My mother hadn't thought to medicate him. So much depends on the questions we ask. *How is he feeling* versus *how are you feeling* is the difference between life and death. I held onto the small white paper as it waved slowly in the wind like a surrender flag. That day dusk didn't arrive. I went into it.

The Situation—died on August 3, 2015, at least part of the situation; my father was the other situation. A situation isn't like a jacket you can just take off the person. The situation is the skin, the body's eggshell, its flowerpot. If you pull the arms off a clock, you still have the clock. Time keeps going because the arms measure time but are not time. To want the situation to die but not the person is like wanting the gallop but not the horse. There are many things I can't put into a box: wind, marvel, time, suffering. I have no answer. I have no more questions. Because *when?* means the situation will be over. My face will carry those of two dead people. And I can finally put down the dictionary.

Memory—died on February 12, 2015. It was a routine. We'd arrive, the children would give my mother a hug, leave the room to watch TV, and I would sit on a small stool ten feet away from the La-Z-Boy chair I had given her. The oxygen machine tired and gurgling, my father pacing in the other room. *Alibaba,* my mother said. *What?* I asked. *Alibaba,* she repeated, *I should buy some.* Again and again she asked me over several weeks as if for the first time. I can still hear her voice, the shrill accented chorus of the *A,* the *li,* then *baba,* the same phrase for father in Chinese. Even as she was dying, she thought the path to God was money. I wonder if she heard coins in her dreams, if when God touched her forehead, his fingertips felt like gold. I bought her the Alibaba shares in March, and it's up 40.64%.

Doctors—died on August 3, 2015. Dr. Lynch, Dr. Chang, Dr. Mahoney, the ER doctors, the nurses, their blank faces as they pulled thin blankets up to my mother's shoulders, the frozen summers. When Dr. Mahoney finally arrived, I forgot all my questions. My heart opened like a tear. He said he was leaving the practice and I wondered why we call groups of doctors a *practice,* as if not yet experts. Maybe because they can't know how to die until they die. When he spoke, I tried not to emit warmth. He wanted to *do something different,* as if saving my mother could be a career option. He talked for twenty minutes. We forgot about my mother in the small bed, just a curtain separating her and the three moaning women. How we go in and out of caring about others. As I returned to my mother's room, I slid down the microscope and felt myself shrinking.

Obsession—born on January 20, 1940, never died after the stroke but grew instead. The stroke gained an oak door, not just hard but impenetrable. The obsessions lived in solitude behind the oak door. After his stroke, the obsession took my father to the gym to walk on the treadmill. He walked as if through a wildfire, he walked so much, he disappeared. His brain now had an accent and no one could understand how to stop him from learning the new language. My mother called and said he fell on the treadmill, hit his head, blood thinners spread his blood like moonlight. They drilled holes in his head, vacuumed out the blood and more words. My father was finally arrested, he turned in the rest of his words, they bound his tongue. And he dreamed in blank paper.

My children, children,
tonight, during a reading,
a white writer said:
She was a squinty-eyed cunt.
My *squinty eyes* remain closed.

*

My children don't have
squinty eyes, they have breathing.
Their breathing sends roads
into the white man's body.
These roads can lead to starlings.

The Clock—died on June 24, 2009 and it was untimely. How many times my father has failed the *clock test.* Once I heard a scientist with Alzheimer's on the radio, trying to figure out why he could no longer draw a clock. It had to do with the *superposition of three types.* The hours represented by 1 to 12, the minutes where a 1 no longer represents 1 but 5, and a 2 now represents 10, then the second hand that measures 1 to 60. I sat at the stoplight and thought of the clock, its perfect circle and its *superpositions,* all the layers of complication on a plane of thought, yet the healthy read the clock in one single instant without a second thought. I think about my father and his lack of first thoughts, how every thought is a second or third or fourth thought, unable to locate the first most important thought. I wonder about the man on the radio and how far his brain has degenerated since. Marvel at how far our brains allow language to wander without looking back but knowing where the pier is. If you unfold an origami swan, and flatten the paper, is the paper sad because it has seen the shape of the swan or does it aspire towards flatness, a life without creases? My father is the paper. He remembers the swan but can't name it. He no longer knows the paper swan represents an animal swan. His brain is the water the animal swan once swam in, holds everything, but when thawed, all the fish disappear. Most of the words we say have something to do with fish. And when they're gone, they're gone.

Hope—died on October 15, 2014 when the FDA approved two drugs, Esbriet and Ofev for pulmonary fibrosis. I did what I was trained to do, researched, read, asked questions. I taped to my wall articles that now look like tombstones. Hope is the wildest bird, the one that flies so fast it will either disappear or burst into flames. My mug from Japan says *Enjoy the Happiness Time.* As if it knows happiness is attached to time somehow. The drugs could slow down the disease but not reverse it. We chose hospice. In my child's homework: *Which of the following happens eventually? a) You are born, b) You die, c) A long winter comes to an end, d) Practice makes perfect.* I no longer know how to answer this.

The Head—died on August 3, 2015. When the two men finally came, they rolled a gurney into the other room, hushed talking and noises, then the tip of the gurney came out like a cruise ship. They were worried about dinging the walls. My mother's whole body covered with a blanket. Her head gone. Her face gone. Rilke was wrong. The body is nothing without the head. My mother, now covered, was no longer my mother. A covered apple is no longer an apple. A sketch of a person isn't the person. Somewhere, in the morning, my mother had become the sketch. And I would spend the rest of my life trying to shade her back in.

The Blue Dress—died on August 6, 2015, along with the little blue flowers, all silent. Once the petals looked up. Now small pieces of dust. I wonder whether they burned the dress or just the body? I wonder who lifted her up into the fire? I wonder if her hair brushed his cheek before it grew into a bonfire? I wonder what sound the body made as it burned? They dyed her hair for the funeral, too black. She looked like a comic character. I waited for the next comic panel, to see the speech bubble and what she might say. But her words never came and we were left with the stillness of blown glass. The irreversibility of rain. And millions of little blue flowers. Imagination is having to live in a dead person's future. Grief is wearing a dead person's dress forever.

Hindsight—never existed until August 3, 2015. Someone had painted over hindsight. But if you paint over something, it still exists. On some nights, while the children brush their teeth, I hide under their blankets and jump out when they return. I try to make myself as flat as possible, try not to move as if I have died. Every time, I run out of air. Every time, I realize I don't want to die. Every time, I realize death doesn't care what I want. Sometimes, a child screams, but most of the time, they see my shape or my foot and know I am alive. I wish I had known exactly when my mother would die. As in an appointment. Then I would have moved my feelings earlier. I wouldn't have painted over her mouth. I wouldn't have painted over my heart. Now that it's over, I know the heart doesn't really shatter, but I also can no longer feel it.

The Priest—died on August 3, 2015.
As he died, he cursed. When the
priest first started coming, he left
a watermark on the door. As time
passed, my mother's door was
riddled with bullets from his fist. He
started sending me prayers with his
eyes. I didn't want his prayers. I had
too many selves for God to save.
None of my selves knew how to say
sorry. None of my selves knew each
other. I wonder if my mother took
God in toward the end? The way she
had once cared for her fifty bonsai
plants each morning, snipping gently,
adjusting tiny sprinklers, beckoning
them with her breath. The bonsai
barely responded, had never asked
to be limited. She said the priest was
weird, would look at her in a creepy
way. As if he knew she was not a
believer, but a refugee. When she
arrived in this country ,they painted
over her skin. Her fungal toes only
looked like roots.

I put on a shirt,
put on a pair of work pants
because I will die.
How the snow falls to its death,
how snow is just dressed-up rain.

*

Where do they find hope?
Sometimes the city has pleats,
sometimes the body
rings with joy shaped like violets,
sometimes the night wind tingles.

The Car—it was difficult work to take away. It died on March 13, 2015. Before my mother died, my father studied for six months for the DMV test, as if it were an entrance exam to heaven. My mother found him old tests in Chinese. He sat at the table, hand to his head, mumbling, walking so many times to my mother's chair, a small river formed under him. *2. God suddenly cuts in front of you creating a hazard. Which of these actions should you take first? a) Honk and step on the brake firmly, b) Take your foot off the gas, c) Swerve into the lane next to you.* Is there a choice *d*? *Accelerate and run God over.*

My Mother's Favorite Potted Tree—
died in 2016, a slow death. The day
I looked up, the pink blossoms gone,
the branches shabby opium pipes.
The pot the only thing recognizable.
I had moved the tree here and it had
died too. My neighbor insisted it was
still living as if insisting could make
it bloom again. His parents were
still alive so I let him believe. One
morning, small black sprinklers in the
pot. I had forgotten about the hope of
others. I had forgotten about others. I
only had one friend left—Death. That
year, I quit my job. When I brushed
my children's hair, birds flew out from
underneath. My mother would not
have approved. I can see her face
as I tell her the wrong story. As time
passes, my memories of her are like
a night animal racing across the roof.
I know it is an animal, but I will never
be able to see it or know when it will
come again.

Similes—died on August 3, 2015. There was nothing like death, just death. Nothing like grief, just grief. How the shadow of a chain-link fence can look like a fish's scales but never be. Once my mother called late at night because she was constipated. The streetlamps still looked like things with their long arched arms. I sat on her bed in the dark. The glow from the bathroom light still like everything. I filled and emptied the plastic sitz bath that looked like something. Her two elbows still able to make small bowls on her knees. I gave her instructions and said nothing more. If only words could represent thought in the way a microphone represents words.

Affection—died on November 12, 1978, the last picture I see of my mother's arms around me. At the funeral, I never touched my sister. When the room was finally empty, she sat in the front row with her spouse. I watched his arm lift and fall onto her shoulder. When my spouse's parents died, both times, he burst into tears, inextinguishable tears that quickly extinguished. The first time, he hugged me and not his family. The second time, he hugged no one. When the nurse called, she said, *I'm sorry, but your mother passed away this morning.* When I told my children, the three of us hugged in a circle, burst *into* tears. As if the tears were already there crying on their own and we, the newly bereaved, exploded into them. In the returning out of the tears, the first person *I* dissolves a little more each time.

Home—died sometime around 1960 when my mother left Taipei. Home died again on August 3, 2015. Home's fingertips trimmed off each time. New stubs became conscious, became heads of state, just shorter and fatter. Now home is a looking glass called Rose Hills Memorial Park. How far she has travelled from Beijing to Taipei to New York to Pennsylvania to Michigan to California to Rose Hills. When a white writer has a character call another a *squinty-eyed cunt,* I search for my mother. I call her name but I can't remember her voice. I think it is squinty. She would have said, *Don't listen to lao mei, we all end up in the same place.* But where is that place? Are there doors there? Cattails? Now there are barbed wires in her throat, her words are stillbirth. All the new flat tombstones since my last visit, little stretchers on the lawn. I lie down next to her stone, close my eyes. I know many things now. Even with my eyes closed, I know a bird passes over me. In hangman, the body forms while it is being hung. As in, we grow as we are dying.

When a mother dies,
a house becomes a forest.
My children, children,
know that I am in the trees.
True love means you won't find me.

*

My children, children,
remember to let me go,
delete my number,
save the number of the trees.
Remember, the lemons speak.

The Bees—268 million years old from the Philippines, passed away on April 26, 2217 in Nome, Alaska. The detaching icebergs crushed the bees who used to fly over conference rooms. Once I nearly died in a small plane with a CEO, CFO, and COO during their IPO. On the ground, the CEO glared at me, as if I had caused the storm. As if the yellow lights had come from my mind. As if the buzzing had come from my shaking. As if the lightning were a box I had tripped over. Maybe he was right. Maybe I had become estranged from a part of myself that wanted to stay alive. That wanted them to remain alive. In the same way I had become estranged from my mother forever, but not from her death.

Victoria Chang—died on August 3, 2015, the one who never used to weep when other people's parents died. Now I ask questions, I bring glasses. I shake the trees in my dreams so I can tremble with others tomorrow. Only one of six siblings came to the funeral, the oldest uncle. A few called and cried or asked questions. This uncle said he knew something had happened because the morning my mother died he felt someone kick him, certain it was her. Now I know others found my mother difficult too. But she was not his mother. She was mine, all mine. Therefore anger towards her was mine. All mine. Anger after someone has died is a cake on a table, fully risen. A knife housed in glass.

Clothes—died on August 10, 2015. We stuffed them into lawn bags to donate. Shirt after shirt, button-down after button-down, dress after dress, limb after limb. A few leapt out to me like the flame from a nightmare, the kind of flame that almost seems human in its gestures. I kept those. I kept the hundreds of pencils. I am writing with a pencil from my mother's drawer. It says *Detroit Public Schools,* where she taught. Each sentence fights me. Once we rolled her downstairs, played croquet and putt-putt golf. She sat and watched, her vacant eyes not seeing anything we saw. As if she were looking beyond us, beyond the sun. The days of August already made a certain way that she could see and we couldn't. I left her in the sun too long. One child doing cartwheels on the grass as my mother looked on, wearing the white blouse with the small pink flowers swirling in a pattern. I kept the stare. I kept the flowers. And I donated the vacant shirt.

Guilt—never died on August 3, 2017.
I hired a hit man to use a missile. But
guilt still lies in a heap on my chest
at night like a pile of frozen pigeons.
Last month, my father fell again and
I walked through him for the third
time. They told me he was trying to
run away and tripped. Another brain
bleed. We moved him upstairs to
memory care, as if strangers could
somehow care for his memory. When
I visited, no one could find him. We
opened one door after another,
the square-tipped smells of each
person rushed out. We found him in
someone else's bed, hair buzzing.
He handed me his glasses and said,
Here's my future. And all I could think
was, *What would my dead mother
do?* I went from room to room looking
for her. All I found were dismembered
shadows and bodies in C shapes,
heads emptied out. I could hear all
of the hearts beating in the dark. The
problem was they all sounded the
same. My own heart slowed. Guilt
had turned into a heart too, mixed in
the pile, breeding with all the other
hearts.

The Ocean—died on August 21, 2017, when I didn't jump from the ship. Instead, I dragged the door shut and pulled up the safety latch. The water in my body wanted to pour into the ocean and I imagined myself being washed by the water, my body separating into the droplets it always was. I could feel the salt on my neck for days. A woman I once knew leapt out of a window to her death. The difference was she was being chased. Some scientists say the ocean is warming. Some say the ocean has hypoxic areas with no oxygen. Even water has hierarchy. A child's death is worse than a woman's death unless the woman who died was the mother of the child and the only parent. If the woman who died was the mother of an adult, it is merely *a part of life.* If both mother and daughter die together, it is *a shame.* If a whole family dies, it is *a catastrophe.* What will we call a whole ocean's death? *Peace.*

The Face—died on August 3, 2015, along with the body, particles of gray dust and small white bones. The face represents a personhood, the part we show to others the most. Could I identify my mother by her hands? Her feet? On the way to JFK, an old cemetery, headstones all different sizes, tilted. The headstone represents a person's face, not in the same way a photo represents a face. A horn means something. It makes us look up and out at the train. When the train leaves, the tracks represent an absence but also imply a train once existed. Imply a hope, a return. Maybe there are no beginnings. Maybe nothing is an elegy, in the way rain from indoors is neither a beginning nor an end.

My children say no,
I say *yes* because I know.
 I tell them they can.
But today, people were shot.
We walk into a blender.

*

Have you ever looked
so closely at a child's face
that you could see God,
see the small hairs that you know
will lift with each new shooting?

IV

The canopy of civilisation is burnt out. The sky is dark as polished whale-bone. But there is a kindling in the sky whether of lamplight or of dawn. There is a stir of some sort— sparrows on plane trees somewhere chirping.

—Virginia Woolf, *The Waves*

America—died on February 14, 2018, and my dead mother doesn't know. Since her death, America has died a series of small deaths, each one less precise than the next. My tears are now shaped like hooks but my heart is damp still. If it is lucky, it is in the middle of its beats. The unlucky dead children hold telegrams they must hand to a woman at a desk. The woman will collect their belongings and shadows. My dead mother asks each of these children if they know me, have seen me, how tall my children are now. They will tell her that they once lived in Florida, not California. She will see the child with the hole in his head. She will blow the dreams out of the hole like dust. I used to think death was a kind of anesthesia. Now I imagine long lines, my mother taking in all the children. I imagine her touching their hair. How she might tickle their knees to make them laugh. The dead hold the other half of our ticket. The dead are an image of wind. And when they comb their hair, our trees rustle.

I am ready to
admit I love my children.
To admit this is
to admit that they will die.
Die: no one knows this but words.

*

My children, children,
this poem will not end because
I am trying to
end this poem with hope hope hope,
see how the mouth stays open?

Notes

During the process of writing the *Obit* poems, I referenced Virginia Woolf's *The Waves* and plucked out occasional words to spark my imagination.

Only after I had written "My Mother's Lungs" did I read *Blue Nights* by Joan Didion and find that she had a similar thought about time change and death.

"I am a miner. The light burns blue" is the first line of Sylvia Plath's poem "Nick and the Candlestick."

The phrase "Imagination is having to live in a dead person's future" in the poem "The Blue Dress" is inspired by Richard Siken's line "I live in someone else's future" from his book *War of the Foxes.*

The phrase "in the way rain from indoors is neither a beginning nor an end" in the poem "The Face" is inspired
by Brian Teare's line "the way from indoors the sound of rain is both figure and ground" from his book *The Empty Form Goes All the Way to Heaven.*

Acknowledgments

Thank you to the editors of the following journals in which many of the poems in this book appeared, often in earlier forms:

The Academy of American Poets Poem-a-Day: "The Blue Dress" and "My Father's Frontal Lobe"

Adroit Journal: "My Mother's Favorite Potted Tree," "Similes,"and "Tomas Tranströmer"

AGNI: "Control" and "Optimism—died of monotony"

Alaska Quarterly Review: "Hindsight" and "Reason"

The American Poetry Review: "Empathy," "Language—It wanted to live, " and "Time"

At Length: "Doctors—Dr. Lynch was supposed to," "Friendships—died a slow death," "Home—died sometime around 1960," "Memory—It was a routine" (as "Money"),"Subject Matter," and "Yesterday"

Blackbird: "Hope" "Victoria Chang—died unknowingly," and "Voice Mail"

The Georgia Review: "Approval" "Language—died again," "The Priest," and "Victoria Chang—the one who never used to weep"

Guernica: "The Future"

Kenyon Review: "Affection" "The Clock," "Clothes," "Friendships—died once beloved," "The Ocean," and "Optimism—died a slow death into a pavement"

Michigan Quarterly Review: "Appetite—Once, in graduate school," "Form—my children sleep," "Hands," "Memory—When I returned," and "Secrets"

Mississippi Review: "Privacy" and "Tears"

Narrative: "Appetite—died its final death," "Doctors—Dr.Lynch, Dr. Chang, Dr. Mahoney," "My Mother," "Oxygen," "The Situation," and "Tankas," published together as a group

New England Review: "Grief," "Memory—The death was not sudden," and "Music"

The Normal School: "The Head—died on August 3" and "Home—died on January 12, 2013"

Ploughshares: "Civility" and "Logic"

Poetry: "Caretakers" and "My Mother' s Teeth"

Poetry London: "Victoria Chang—died unwillingly" and "The Car"

A Public Space: "The Face"

Shenandoah: "Gait" and "My Mother's Lungs"

Terrain.org: "America"

32 Poems: "The Doctors—died surrounded by" and "Obsession"

Tin House: "Form—After my mother died," "Sadness," and "Victoria Chang—died at the age of 41"

West Branch: "Ambition" and "Chair"

The Yale Review: "The Bees" and "Guilt"

Many sections of "I Am a Miner. The Light Burns Blue." were published separately in different forms in journals such as *AGNI, Blackbird, Cerise Press, Gulf Coast, Harvard Review, The Journal, Kenyon Review, Meridian, New England Review, Pleiades, The Southeast Review,* and *The Southern Review.*

"Affection," "The Clock," "Clothes," "Friendships—died once beloved," "The Ocean," and "Optimism—died a slow death into a pavement"—all poems published in the *Kenyon Review*— also appeared in *Best American Poetry 2019,* selected by Major Jackson and published by Scribner.

"Language—died, brilliant and beautiful" was anthologized in *The Eloquent Poem*, edited by Elise Paschen and published by Persea Books.

A part of this book was awarded the Poetry Society of America's 2018 Alice Fay di Castagnola Award. "The Obituary Writer" was published on PSA's website.

Thank you to Copper Canyon Press and the entire team.

Thank you to the Guggenheim Foundation, the Sustainable Arts Foundation, the Poetry Society of America, the Pushcart Prize, the Housatonic Book Awards, the Lannan Foundation,and the MacDowell Colony for support and encouragement.

Thanks to all my beloved friends and supporters—way too many to mention, but here are just a few: Ilya Kaminsky (for tirelessly reading many versions of the manuscript and for all the conversations), G. C. Waldrep + Dana Levin + John Gallaher (my trusted friends in art and life), Dean Rader, Rick Barot, David Baker, Isaac Fitzgerald, Liza Voges, Jen Chang,Maggie Smith, Ann Townsend, and Wayne Miller; my LA poet friends Van Khanna, Blas Falconer, Elline Lipkin, and Charlie Jensen; my National Book Critics Circle colleagues; all my Antioch University colleagues (thanks Bernadette,Natalie, and Daisy!); my Idyllwild colleagues such as Ed Skoog and Heather Companiott; all my social media friends,and so many more...

Thanks to my family for tolerating my obsession with poetry and poems. Thanks to my wiener dogs, Mustard and Ketchup, for listening to me read all these poems aloud a billion times. Thank you to my father, who unknowingly has populated my poems for the last decade, and finally, thank you to my mother, whom I've never properly thanked.

226

About the Author

Victoria Chang's prior books are *Barbie Chang, The Boss, Salvinia Molesta,* and *Circle.* Her children's picture book, *Is Mommy?,* was illustrated by Marla Frazee and published by Beach Lane Books/Simon & Schuster. It was named a Notable Book by the *New York Times.* Her middle grade novel, *Love Love,* was published by Sterling Publishing. She has received a Guggenheim Fellowship, a Sustainable Arts Foundation Fellowship, the Poetry Society of America's Alice Fay di Castagnola Award, a Pushcart Prize, a Lannan Residency Fellowship, and a MacDowell Colony Fellowship. She lives in Los Angeles and is the program chair of Antioch's low-residency MFA program.

经 典 照 亮 前 程